Neighbours ™

Ramsay street, Erinsborough. May 13, 1975.
  It started out like any morning at the Robinson house.
Nothing to single it out from any other. Anne Robinson,
eight months pregnant, was in her dressing gown cooking
eggs and bacon at the stove. Her husband, Jim, was reading
the newspaper. Scott, seven, sprawled on the floor with a
comic. Paul 12, and Julie, 11 were having their usual breakfast squabble.
  Little did Jim know that this was the day that would change
the rest of his life.

Neighbours™

THE ROBINSONS
A FAMILY IN CRISIS!

Written by
VALDA MARSHALL

Based on the **Grundy Television Series**
as shown on BBC Television

Mandarin

A Mandarin Paperback

NEIGHBOURS 2

First published in Great Britain 1989
by Mandarin Paperbacks
Michelin House, 81 Fulham Road, London SW3 6RB

Mandarin is an imprint of the Octopus Publishing Group

Neighbours™ & © 1989 Grundy Television Pty Limited

A CIP catalogue record for this book is available from
the British Library.

ISBN 0 7493 0056 6

Printed in Great Britain by Cox & Wyman Ltd, Reading

Chapter 1

RAMSAY street, Erinsborough. May 13, 1975.
It started out like any morning at the
Robinson house. Nothing to single it out from
any other. Anne Robinson, eight months pregnant, was in her dressing gown cooking eggs
and bacon at the stove. Her husband, Jim, was
reading the newspaper. Scott, seven, sprawled
on the floor with a comic. Paul, 12, and Julie,
11 were having their usual breakfast squabble.

Little did Jim know that this was the day that
would change the rest of his life.

It had started in a panic, because both Jim
and Anne had slept in. Anne, her stomach bulging with her fourth child, had had a restless
night, tossing and turning to try and relieve the
cramps in her legs. Jim, lying alongside her in
the oldfashioned wooden double bed that had
been a wedding present from Anne's mother
Helen, was also finding it hard to sleep.

It wasn't just Anne's restlessness that was

keeping him awake. He was also going over in his mind the speech he was to give next day at the engineering conference. The address was originally to be given by his departmental head Richard Collingwood. But at the last minute Richard had gone down with 'flu, and had asked Jim to take over for him. Jim was confident about the technical details, and knew his subject, but was nervous at speaking before so many of his peers. The words kept going around and around in his head.

Finally he got out of bed, and padded through to the kitchen to make cups of hot cocoa for himself and Anne. Maybe that would help the two of them get to sleep.

But when he brought the two cups back to bed, they stayed awake talking about the coming baby and their plans for the future.

What would they call this one? And should they add another bedroom to the house?

Although the other three had been planned, this new one had come as a surprise. Not unwelcome, because both Jim and Anne loved children. Jim had been an only child, and remembered the loneliness of it. Anne had also been the only one, until her parents adopted a baby girl, Rosemary. They wanted their children to grow up in the warmth and closeness of a large family.

As they talked, Jim leaned over and put an arm across Anne.

"Hey, I felt it!" he said. "The little beggar gave me a kick."

Anne smiled and put her hand over his.

"It's a lot more active than the other ones," she said. "I think it's going to be early."

They talked through names again, trying once more to decide on one. If it was a boy, Jim wanted to call it James after his father — Captain James Robinson, killed during World War II. His mother Bess would like that. Anne was certain the baby would be another girl, and favoured something oldfashioned like Alice or Lucy. They talked until just before dawn, then fell asleep. Neither heard the alarm when it went off.

It wasn't until Julie hammered on the door at eight, demanding to know why breakfast was late, that they woke. Then it was a mad scramble for the bathroom and shower, with Anne preparing breakfast as Jim dressed for the conference.

At the breakfast table, Paul and Julie were arguing about whose turn it was to clear the dishes. Since Anne had been pregnant, Jim had drawn up a work roster to help lighten the domestic load. Everyone had regular jobs, even Scott. The roster was taped to the refrigerator door, and Jim made sure it was followed scrupulously.

The squabble this time was because Paul had missed on his morning chores because of football practice, and Julie was complaining she'd had to do extra work.

"I can't help it if I had to go early," said Paul. "The coach made me."

"Well then, you should do two days at washing up," retorted Julie. "You're always getting out of things, because of football or something stupid. It's not fair, and you know it."

"Bossy britches," taunted Paul. He knew she hated being called that.

Julie turned pink with anger, and appealed to her father.

"It's not fair, dad," she said. "Just because he's a boy, he gets away with anything. Why does it have to be my turn again today?"

Jim looked across at Anne, and they exchanged smiles. These breakfast spats between Julie and Paul were a regular breakfast feature, and they were used to it. Scott, on the other hand, rarely fought with anyone. He had been a quiet, placid baby, and had grown into a sunny-tempered boy.

When Julie was only four years old, Anne had caught her staggering around the bedroom with her infant brother in her arms. Anne had

4

rushed over to grab the baby from her, fearful Julie would let him fall. Even at that early age, Julie had shown the mothering instinct. Anne knew when this new baby came, Julie would be a great help. Jim, too, had a soft spot for his only daughter.

"Never mind, Princess," he said, putting an arm around her. "Tell you what, I'll give you a hand."

Jim was just putting the dishes into the sink, when Max Ramsay walked through the back door. Max was their next door neighbour, and Jim's oldest friend. They'd been to school together, but had lost touch when Jim went to University to study engineering and Max had become a plumber. Jim heard he'd moved to Queensland with his family. Later, another schoolmate mentioned Max had married the daughter of an Italian migrant.

It had been a pleasant surprise to Jim, then, when he found himself living in the same street as his childhood pal. Not that he should have been too surprised by it. The street had been named after Max's grandfather Jack, an early pioneer orchardist in the area, and at school Max used to brag that one day some of the land would be his.

"Kids want a lift to school?" asked Max. "The van's about ready to go."

Going to school in Uncle Max's plumber's van had long been a treat for the Robinson children. They would pile in the back with Shane and Danny Ramsay, squeezing themselves in among the pipes and work equipment, and waving to their less fortunate friends who had to walk.

But now that they were getting older, and Paul had started High School, the novelty was beginning to wear off. Paul said he'd give it a miss, and walk with Shane. Julie was at a stage where she felt it wasn't ladylike to be seen in the back of a van. Only Scott and Danny still got a kick out of it.

Jim poured Max a cup of coffee, while Anne hustled the kids to get ready. Schoolbooks, lunches, raincoats, clean shoes, clean handkerchiefs. At the last minute Scott remembered he had to take money for a school outing. Anne went off to the bedroom to get it.

Max looked after her with undisguised admiration.

"Don't know how she does it," he said. "Just about ready to drop her bundle, and she's still on the go. She's an amazing woman."

Jim agreed. Although all four pregnancies had been relatively trouble-free, Anne had never been one to ease up on her workload. She was an organised person, calm and efficient, and ran the Robinson household like clockwork.

Meals were on the table on time, Jim could always rely on clean shirts and socks in his drawer, and the children went off to school each morning bright and shiny as new coins.

"How's the swimming going?" asked Jim. Max was a sports fanatic, and had been a champion sprinter when they were both at school. A pulled tendon had put paid to any chance of going further, and Max had given away all idea of competitive running. But Shane, his elder son, was showing promise as a swimmer and diver . . . and Max spent all his spare time coaching him.

"I'm entering him for under-12s in backstroke," said Max.

"He's also going to have a go at the high dive."

"How about Danny?" asked Jim. As soon as he got the words out, he knew he'd touched on a sensitive subject. Danny, the younger, was a rebel and a tearaway. Max had a short fuse at the best of times, but Danny tested his temper. Jim sometimes felt that Max was unfair to his second son, and favoured Shane over him. Shane's swimming ability was one example. Although Danny had done moderately well at the school championships, Max's only thoughts had been to coach Shane to Olympic standards. And from the odd remark let drop by Scott, Danny's closest friend, Jim knew Danny resented it.

"Him?" snorted Max in disgust. "He'd be pushed to win in the dog paddle. Lacks concentration, that's his trouble . . . fools around too much. The trouble is, Maria spoils him. He's just a mummy's boy."

"Max, he's only seven," protested Jim mildly. "Give the kid a chance."

But Max didn't want to talk any more about his troublesome younger son. As Anne came back into the room and gave Scott his money, he got up to go.

"Okay, let's get cracking," he said. Scott raced out the door, swinging his schoolbag. Paul and Julie followed at a more leisurely pace.

Outside the front of the Ramsay house, young Danny was already in the ute. Scott climbed in alongside him, as Max got into the driver's seat.

"Sure you kids won't want to change your mind?" he asked, as Shane emerged from the house. Julie shook her head, and started walking. She had a friend Sarah who lived nearby, and the two usually went to school together. As Jim came out and watched her go, he thought once again of how much she looked like Anne. She was Anne in miniature . . . petite, pretty, very feminine. Julie had never been a tomboy, preferring her dolls and teasets to climbing trees or romping with the boys. Jim knew that when she grew up, she would be exactly like her mother.

Shane and Paul turned down Max's offer, and went off together down the street. They were good mates, although Shane wouldn't be starting High School until next year. They'd virtually grown up together, ever since Max built his house next door to the Robinsons.

Anne came out, and Jim put an arm around her as Max drove off with Danny and Scott in the back, waving as they disappeared around the corner.

"We're so lucky," said Anne, leaning against Jim's shoulder. "Three children, and all happy and healthy. I hope this next one is the same."

"It will be," said Jim, as they walked slowly back into the house. On the way, he stopped to inspect some rose bushes he'd just planted. Roses were Anne's favourite flower. She'd carried a bouquet of white roses at their wedding, and every year on their anniversary Jim made a point of giving her the same.

When they'd bought the house, a single-storied red brick with tiled roof and three bedrooms, it had been brand new with no garden. Just weeds, and some builder's rubbish, with a concrete driveway leading to the garage under the house.

The house was in a new development in Ramsay street, a crescent-shaped area cut off from the rest of Ramsay street by a main highway. It was this that appealed to Jim and Anne when they first inspected Number 26. There would only be half a dozen houses in the crescent, and because there was no through traffic it would be perfect for children. They could ride their tricycles and scooters on the footpatch in safety.

Number 28 nextdoor was just being built, and Number 26 was still an empty block. Jim liked the idea of being in a small community, where neighbours were also friends. So did Anne. They stretched their budget, took out a bank loan, and bought the house.

When they moved in, Jim and Anne had spent all their weekends getting the garden into shape, clearing out builder's rubbish, buying topsoil, and planting it with flowers and shrubs. Jim enjoyed the hard physical work, he found it relaxing after a week sitting at a desk. Anne, who had inherited her mother's artistic nature, liked planning the beds of annuals so that each year they burst into a riot of colour.

The Robinson house was never without a vase of freshly-picked flowers, and the younger children took small bouquets to their favourite teachers.

Back in the kitchen, Jim and Anne sat down

for a quiet last cup of coffee together. These were the moments they cherished, with the place to themselves and no one else around.

"Nervous about the speech?" asked Anne.

This was the first time Jim had addressed a major conference, and she knew he was anxious to make it good. His boss had given him the rough notes he'd prepared, but he'd told Jim to feel free to change it to suit himself. So long as the major points were put across, and the department's policy presented, it didn't matter if Jim used his own words. So Jim had been rewriting and polishing and rehearsing, until now he had it word perfect.

"I'll be fine," said Jim. "I'm looking forward to it, actually. By the way, don't worry if I'm a bit late for dinner. These things tend to drag on a bit."

"I'll keep it warm for you," said Anne. "It's a casserole, it will stay hot in the oven."

Jim looked at his watch, and reacted when he saw the time. He grabbed his briefcase, and kissed Anne goodbye.

"Now take it easy, and don't go overdoing it," he said.

"I don't want you to tire yourself out. Why don't you go back to bed for the rest of the morning?"

Anne pulled a face.

"Stop being a fusspot," she said. I'm fine, truly. Besides, mum said she might call in later after her art class, and go shopping. She's going to buy a new dress, and she wants me to come along to give an opinion."

"Why don't you get one for yourself at the same time," suggested Jim.

Anne looked at her bulging figure, and laughed.

"You mean, buy a tent?" she asked.

Jim gave her an affectionate hug, as he got up to leave.

"You're not going to look like that forever," he said. "Get yourself something nice and glamorous, and I'll take you out to dinner when you come home from hospital. Helen can babysit, she won't mind."

Helen was Helen Daniels, Anne's widowed mother. She lived in a small flat not far from them, and was a tower of strength in times of family crisis. Her husband Bill had died soon after Scott was born, and Helen had transferred her energies from looking after a sick husband to looking after her grandchildren. She enjoyed baby sitting, and the children loved having "Gran" around.

When Anne went into hospital to have her fourth child, Helen would be moving in to keep the place running until her return.

"I'll think about it," said Anne. "The dress, I mean . . . not the dinner. I'll take you up on that. But I'd rather buy something when I can see my own feet."

Jim kissed Anne again, as he picked up his briefcase with the notes for the conference.

"Give Helen my love," he said. "Tell her she's my favourite mother-in-law."

Anne smiled back, as Jim walked out the door.

"I'll tell her," she said.

Jim had always got on well with Helen right from the start of their marriage. Anne was grateful for that, knowing what kind of problems there could sometimes be in family relationships. Her mother had been loving and supportive, even when her father Bill had worried about his teenage daughter marrying a penniless University student. She had helped them through Anne's first pregnancy, minding Paul while Anne did part-time jobs to pay the bills. And she was still a Rock of Gibraltar when things went wrong.

To Jim, Helen had always been more of a friend than a mother-in-law. He admired her intelligence and independence, and they shared a common interest in world affairs and politics. Anne would often sit with her mending, amused, as Jim and Helen vehemently battled out some issue.

Anne and Jim were of different temperaments . . . Anne quiet and placid, rarely pushed to anger; Jim the more volatile. But there was one thing on which they were both in total agreement — Helen Daniels was a special kind of person.

Chapter 2

"VERY nice . . . very nice indeed, Mrs. Daniels," commented Lawrence Manning as he peered over Helen's shoulder to look at her painting. "That shows real promise!"

It was the Wednesday morning art class at the Community Centre, and Helen was putting the finishing touches to a delicate water colour of the Robinson garden. She had done the painting from a photo taken the previous spring, when the beds were ablaze with phlox, petunias and zinnias, and had added a personal touch . . . Anne in her wide-brimmed gardening hat, a bunch of flowers in her arms.

Lawrence Manning was a distinguished painter now in his late seventies. He had exhibited at major galleries both in Australia and overseas, but failing eyesight had forced him to give up his career. Nowadays he concentrated on teaching.

Most of the Wednesday morning class were

housewives or retired people, who had taken up painting as a hobby. They were a mixed group, all ages, and with different levels of talent. Helen was one of the star pupils.

"Thanks," said Helen, "But I'm still worried about that bit of sky in the corner. D'you think it's too blue?"

Manning peered again at the painting, frowning.

"No, I don't think so," he said. "I like the contrast. Keep it in, but try another colour for the hat. It's too obtrusive, it detracts from the rest of the picture."

He passed on to the next student, a middle-aged man who had joined the group only recently.

"Not bad . . . not bad at all, Mr. Barrington. Keep at it," he said, then moved away to a young woman in her twenties who was struggling with a still life of a bowl of fruit. David Barrington smiled at Helen.

"He's right, y'know," he said. "That painting of yours is wonderful. I only wish I could do half as well."

Helen smiled back.

"Give it time," she said. "You've hardly started. It's taken me years to get this far."

"Sometimes I wonder why I'm doing it," said David. "I should've picked something easy, like woodwork. At least I'd know a bit about it. But the course sounded interesting, and I thought I'd give it a go.''

"He's a good teacher," said Helen, nodding towards Manning. The best. I've seen some of his work, it's outstanding. He has paintings hanging in London and New York . . . it's a pity he had to give it up."

"You've been to London?" asked David, as he mixed some colours.

Helen laughed.

"Only wish I had," she said. "I'd give anything to be able to see some of those galleries . . . imagine wandering through the Louvre."

"I did once," said David. "Back in 1969. I remember we looked at the Mona Lisa, and were surprised how small it was.''

Helen wondered idly about the "we". David Barrington had never mentioned a wife, and always came and left on his own. Perhaps he was referring to a business associate.

The bell rang for the end of the lesson, just as Helen dropped her brush. She leaned down to pick it up, and bumped heads with David who was doing the same. They both laughed, as David handed it to her.

"My brush with fame," he quipped "I'm sure you're going to be hanging in the Louvre yourself one of these days."

Helen pulled a face. "I don't think I'm quite up to that standard," she said. "I'll be happy if I can produce something that someone wants to hang on their wall."

As they were packing up their equipment, David asked Helen if she lived nearby. She mentioned the address, and said she usually walked. It was a pleasant, brisk ten minute stroll and she enjoyed the exercise. But when they got outside, they found it was raining.

"Let me give you a lift," said David. "I have the car, and go right past your place. It would be a pleasure."

When they arrived at Helen's block of flats, it was still raining but had eased to a drizzle. David had an umbrella in the car, and was going to escort her to the front door. Helen hesitated a moment, then asked if he'd like to come in for coffee. It wasn't something she usually did with people she didn't know well, but he seemed pleasant and interesting. She also sensed he was lonely. Her feelings were confirmed when he accepted instantly, almost as though he'd been hoping for the invitation. He put a hand under her elbow as he steered her to the door, then held her painting bag as she searched for the key.

"It's only small, I'm afraid," Helen apologised, as they went in. "It's all I could af-

18

ford when my husband died.''

David looked around as they entered. Although it was small, as Helen said, it had the unmistakable touch of someone who loved beautiful things. There were good prints on the wall . . . Cezanne, Renoir, an early Hans Heysen. The furniture was comfortable and well-used, and a small side table held a blue vase of flowers. In a glass cabinet were pieces of china, and although David wasn't an expert he could tell they were good. Along one wall was a bookshelf, filled with books that looked as though they'd been read and loved. There was a workbasket with some knitting, that Helen cleared away to make room on the couch.

''For my daughter,'' she explained. ''She's having a baby, and I'm making a shawl.''

''The first?'' asked David.

''The fourth,'' said Helen.

''If it's the fourth, won't your daughter already have plenty of things?'' asked David, as he settled himself down.

''Yes, but I'm determined to make something new,'' said Helen. ''Anyway, I like knitting . . . I find it relaxing. And you know what they say about babies, you can never have too many clothes.''

''I wouldn't know,'' said David. ''We couldn't have any.''

That "we" again . . .

"I'm sorry," said Helen. "It must be sad for your wife."

"Was," amended David. "Janet died three years ago."

As Helen made coffee, David told her a bit more about himself. An accountant, he had taken early retirement from his firm at 55, but still did some part-time consultancy work. One of the reasons for his early retirement had been his wife's health; she had developed cancer. The trip to Paris and the Louvre had been during a world trip they'd taken while the cancer was in remission. But it had come back, and she had finally died.

"I wanted to die myself," said David frankly. "I couldn't handle it, life without Janet. We'd always been so close. Once I even got as far as planning it, but then I decided Janet wouldn't want it. She'd want me to go on — she was that kind of person. So much courage and vitality, even at the last. She didn't believe in giving up."

Janet touched his hand in sympathy, as she handed him the coffee and some home-made cake.

"I'm sorry," she said.

"When I think how much guts that woman had, even when she was suffering, it makes me ashamed," said David. "D'you know what I did when she died — got on the bottle. I used to just sit there night after night, drinking myself silly. That's when I got the idea of killing myself."

"I sat there one night, tossing back the scotch, and I looked at a bottle of sleeping pills. The doctor prescribed them after the funeral, because I couldn't sleep nights."

"I thought to myself, all I have to do is take these pills and finish this bottle of scotch, and it'll all be over. The end . . . finish."

"But you didn't," said Helen.

"I did. But before the stuff could work, I threw up. Sick as a dog all over the place . . . God, what a mess."

He smiled grimly at the memory.

"It was the turning point . . . I decided from then on just to try and get on with my life. Somehow I had to get through it."

"It was my doctor who suggested the art classes. He said it would be good therapy, snap me out of my depression and get my mind off Janet. Some lock themselves up in a room . . . some stare at goldfish . . . me, I just paint badly."

"I know what you mean," sympathised Helen. "It took me a long time to get over Bill."

David held out his cup for a refill, and grinned.

"Here I am, boring the life out of you with all my problems, and you've got plenty of your own. Tell me about your husband."

Helen didn't always find it easy to talk about her late husband, not even with her family. But this pleasant-looking man with the kind face and unassuming manner had opened the floodgates of Helen's memories. She told him how she had married at sixteen, straight from school, after an incident when she had been falsely accused of stealing money from one of her fellow students at a Queensland boarding school.

The real culprit had been her sister Gwen, two years younger. She had borrowed the money from another girl's locker, meaning to put it back. But before she could, the loss of the money was discovered, and Helen was blamed for it. She was shamed before the school assembly, and expelled.

What had hurt Helen most at the time was that her parents didn't believe her. The only one to stand by her was her childhood sweetheart Bill Daniels. They'd always intended to marry when Helen left school, and the expulsion precipitated her into an early wedding. She never went home again.

"And what about Gwen?" asked David.

Helen's normally happy face darkened.

"We don't have anything to do with each

other," she said. "She lives her life, I live mine
. . . and that's the way I like it. I can't ever for-
give what she did to me."

David looked at his watch, and jumped to his
feet.

"Good heavens, I lost track of time. I'm due
for a business appointment in an hour . . . that's
what happens when you start talking about the
past."

"They say it's a sign of getting old," laughed
Helen, as she walked to the door with him.
"But I've enjoyed it."

David paused at the door, and looked at her.

"I've enjoyed it too," he said. "I don't mix
much socially these days, it's nice to talk to
someone again. Especially as we've both been
through the same mill, so to speak."

He stood there, reluctant to leave.

"Would you consider dinner one night?" he
asked. "Say, Friday?"

Helen hesitated. She knew he was probably
just asking her out through loneliness, for someone to talk to. She liked him, and she sensed he
liked her too.

But on the other hand, she hadn't dated a
man since Bill had died six years ago. And although there was nothing in it at this stage, she
was still worried where it could lead.

What if he became serious? What if he

wanted more than friendship, and she couldn't handle it? Then Helen decided she was being silly, and reading too much into a simple dinner invitation.

"I'd love to," she said. And with those words sealed her fate.

Like son-in-law Jim, this would be a day that Helen Daniels would long remember.

Chapter 3

"GOOD lord . . . Jim Robinson, isn't it?"
Jim was walking through the groups of
delegates, trying to find his seat, when he was
stopped by a man whose face was vaguely familiar. The man put out a hand, and grinned.

"Ross Warner. Engineering, 1964."

At once it all clicked into place for Jim. Ross
had been one of the students in his engineering
course at University. He hadn't been a close
friend, but they'd knocked around together in
the same group. Jim remembered Ross as something of a livewire, always getting up petitions
and supporting causes. He'd been on the Student Representative Council, and a co-editor of
the University magazine. Jim, on the other
hand, with a young wife and baby, had all he
could do to cope with his workload. Extracurricular activities such as clubs and University
politics were out for him. He remembered Ross
razzing him about it, asking him if he was plan-

ning to major in nappy-changing.

The years had been kind to Ross. He was a little thicker around the waist, but his hair was as dark and as thick as ever and he had the same cheeky grin.

"I see you're down for an address," said Ross, looking at the program. "Made the big-time, eh?"

"Not really," said Jim. "I'm filling in for my boss, who's sick. What are you doing here?"

"Observer," said Ross. "Just sitting and listening and taking it all in. I'm consultant to a few companies. Say, how about we get together for a drink afterwards, and catch up on old times? And don't tell me you're still changing nappies."

"Almost right," grinned Jim. "Yes, I'd like that. I'll see you later."

Jim moved on and found his seat. Then he took out his speech and studied it again. He felt confident about it, and knew he could do a good job. And he was oddly pleased that Ross Warner of all people was there to hear him.

At University, Ross had been the one to be centre of attention — the brash livewire who was always jumping up and challenging tutors and lecturers. Jim had made his mark with academic excellence, hardworking and dedicated . . . the quiet achiever.

26

When Jim finally stood up to make his speech, he half expected Ross to get to his feet and interrupt with a cry of "Rubbish . . . rubbish!" as in the old days. Instead, Ross sat there quietly listening, making an occasional note.

"Very impressive," commented Ross later, as they made their way to a nearby pub for a beer. "Congratulations."

"Thanks," said Jim.

They settled themselves into a booth, and began catching up on the years. Ross had done extremely well for himself, as Jim thought he would. He was consultant to several companies, and had had a couple of overseas trips. His last one had been to Tokyo, to set up links with a Japanese company. Ross was married, but had no children . . . whether by choice, or for some other reason, he didn't volunteer. He told Jim his wife's name was Margaret, and she had been a secretary with one of the companies which employed him. They'd been married five years.

"I took my time," said Ross, with a grin. "Not like you, you cradle-snatcher. So how many d'you have now?"

Jim told Ross about his family, and the fourth baby they were expecting.

"You're a beggar for punishment, that's all I can say," said Ross. "You must like kids."

"I do," said Jim. "So does Anne. She's a wonderful mother.''

''It must cost you a fortune to feed a mob like that, what kind of money d'you make?'' asked Ross.

Jim explained that his job with a Government department didn't pay the kind of money Ross was earning from private enterprise, but it was safe and secure with good prospects for promotion. In time, if he kept his nose clean and worked hard, he would probably take over as department head. At 65 he would retire with superannuation.

As he talked, Jim was acutely aware of how dull and boring this must sound to Ross Warner. It was beginning to sound boring to himself.

''Funny,'' said Ross. ''Somehow I never imagined you working for the Government. You were always the bright one at Uni, coming up with all the ideas. Remember that car engine you were working on?''

Jim grinned, remembering. He had struggled with the engine for two years, then finally abandoned it.

''That was one that didn't work,'' he said ruefully. ''Otherwise I might now be a millionaire, instead of just a humble public servant.''

Ross looked thoughtful.

''Ever thought of going into business for yourself?'' he asked.

Jim shrugged. "Who doesn't?" he said. "But I'd be mad to take a risk like that, with a wife and family dependent on me."

"It wouldn't be so much of a risk if you had a partner," said Ross. "Someone to share the work and responsibility."

Jim stared at his former colleague, not sure what he was saying. Ross rushed on in a burst of enthusiasm, the words tumbling over each other, as he outlined his plan.

"I've been wanting to set myself up for some time now, and the only thing holding me back has been the right person to work with."

"Running into you today was a stroke of luck . . . almost fate, you might say. We'd be the perfect partnership, don't you see that, Jim? I'd run the business and marketing side, I've got plenty of contacts. The engineering would be all yours. We'd go into it on an equal basis, fifty-fifty. So what d'you say?"

Jim was too stunned at first to answer. Then as the full impact of what Ross was saying began to get through, he shook his head.

"You're asking me to toss in my job," he said. "I couldn't do it."

But Ross wouldn't be put off. He kept talking persuasively, outlining the advantages, pointing out that Jim was still a comparatively young man in his thirties and shouldn't allow himself to be bogged down in a dead-end job. Sure there'd be risks, but they'd both be sharing them. And Ross had done his homework well . . . Jim had to give him that. He produced facts and figures to back up his belief that within twelve months Jim would be making more money than he was now. What's more, if they could develop a few new ideas, the possibilities for expansion would be endless. They could both finish up rich men.

Jim felt himself being swayed by Ross's enthusiasm, and finally had to admit he was interested. But there was still Anne. He told Ross they never made a major decision without first talking it through with each other. It was a pact they made at their marriage.

"All right then, go home and talk it over," said Ross.

"Let me know as soon as possible. But I've got a feeling this is going to work out for both of us. We'll make a great team."

They shook hands, and parted, after Ross gave Jim his address and phone number.

Ross Warner's infectious enthusiasm stayed with Jim for the drive home, as he started thinking of new projects and new ideas. Owning his own engineering plant was something he'd always dreamed about, but never thought possible. And he knew enough about Ross to be confident he would be a good business manager.

It wasn't until he turned into his driveway that the enthusiasm started to wear off. Was he taking on too much, a family man with three children and another on the way? Should he play safe, and stick with his dull but secure Government job? And most of all, what would Anne's reaction be?

Frowning, Jim parked the car and walked into the house.

Chapter 4

ANNE was in the kitchen, showing Julie how to cream butter and sugar for a sponge cake. Paul and Scott were sprawled on the living room floor watching television, but jumped to their feet as soon as they heard their father come in. How did his speech go? Did he get more applause then anyone else?

"I think I passed," said Jim, smiling at Anne over their heads. He decided now wasn't the time to broach the subject of Ross Warner's partnership offer, he'd bring it up later.

"Max came over," said Anne. "Something about going to the beach, but he said it wasn't urgent. Just to tell you to put your head in when you're free. And your dinner's in the oven."

"I'm not so hungry," said Jim. "I think I'll go and see what Max wants."

Anne went back to Julie's cooking lesson, as Jim went through the gate they'd put in their rear dividing fence to give both families quick and easy access.

Max was sitting in the kitchen, feet up, having a beer, as Jim walked in. He offered one to Jim, who shook his head.

"Anne said you wanted to see me?"

"Yeah," said Max. "I thought we might take the kids to the beach this weekend. Bit of salt-water swimming will do Shane good, toughen up his muscles. And he could do with a change of pace, he's been at the pool all week." Jim noticed that Max didn't refer to Danny.

"Okay by me," said Jim. "I'll check with Anne."

Max's wife Maria came in, and started clearing away the dishes. She smiled warmly when she saw Jim, and offered him some coffee. Jim accepted; he always liked the coffee Maria made. It was a special blend that she bought from a nearby Italian delicatessen.

Maria was half Italian. Her father, Franco Rossini, was a tiler who had worked with Max on building jobs in Queensland. She had her father's dark good looks and warm, vibrant personality. But her accent came from her mother, a Czech who had been sent after the war to a refugee camp in Italy.

Maria's father was now dead, the result of falling from a roof while building a house. The mother still lived in Queensland, with a younger daughter Anna.

Jim liked Maria, and so did Anne. They had become close friends since the Ramsays moved next door to them. But the marriage was a volatile one, and there were frequent arguments. The two kitchens were close together, and Jim and Anne could often hear Max's voice bellowing from it.

"Poor Maria," Anne would say. "I wonder what's gone wrong now?"

Right now everything seemed calm, as Max opened another tinnie and Maria offered Jim a piece of her chocolate cake. Like her coffee, she was famous for her chocolate cake, a rich dark one layered with raspberry jam, made from a European recipe brought to Australia by her mother.

"I shouldn't but I will," said Jim, smiling at Maria as she handed it to him.

Danny came racing into the room, yelling and dive bombing with a model aircraft he'd just made. Not for the first time, Jim thought how unalike the two Ramsay brothers were. Shane was tall for his age, blond, with the look of a young Viking. He had a sunny nature, and nothing bothered him. Danny, whom Shane affectionately called "Squirt," was completely different . . . small, dark, thin and wiry, a bundle of energy. He looked nothing like Jim remembered Max at the same age; Jim supposed he probably took after Maria's side of the family.

"Watch it, you clumsy clot!" shouted Max, as Danny dive bombed too close and the can of beer was knocked to the floor. Maria picked it up, and gently shooed Danny back to the other room with Shane. But Jim could sense her irritation at the tone of Max's voice.

"Is Anne busy?" asked Maria. "I've made something for the baby, and I thought I'd take it over."

"Go ahead, she'd love to see you," said Jim.

Anne and Julie were putting the sponge cake into the oven, as Maria knocked and walked in the back door.

"Now no peeking for twenty minutes," Anne was saying. "Go back to your homework, and I'll call you."

Maria watched, envious, as Julie scampered back to her room.

"You're so lucky having a daughter," she sighed. "I'd love to have someone to pass on all the things my mother taught me."

"It's not too late," said Anne, smiling.

A hint of a shadow flickered across Maria's face, and she tensed. Then she was back to her normal, smiling self.

"Two's enough," she said, "Although I

wouldn't mind if I could be guaranteed it would be a girl. A daughter would be good for Max . . . make him a little softer and more understanding. But with my luck, I'd have another boy. No, I think we'll stay the way we are . . . I haven't got your patience, Anne. I'm not sure I could cope any more with all those sleepless nights. Which reminds me . . ."

"She held up a baby's nightie, hand-embroidered and edged with lace.

". . . for the new little Robinson, boy or girl. I finished making it this afternoon."

Anne gave Maria a warm hug, as she took the tiny garment and held it up.

"It's beautiful," she said. "It's too good to use everyday . . . I'll save it for the christening."

"Have you decided on names yet . . . or shouldn't I ask?" said Maria.

"James if it's a boy, that's definite," replied Anne.

"And if it's a girl we're going for something oldfashioned, like Alice or Lucy . . . or maybe Amy. I also like Bess, but Jim won't hear of it."

"What's wrong with Bess?" asked Maria. "I remember when I started school here, they taught us all about Good Queen Bess. It's got a nice sound to it."

"It's also the name of Jim's mother, and

they're not exactly on close terms," said Anne.

Maria looked surprised.

"I've never heard the children mention another grandmother," she said. "I don't know why, but somehow I've always had the impression that both Jim's parents were dead."

"The reason you never hear about her is that she's hardly ever around," said Anne dryly. "In fact, she was hardly ever around when Jim was growing up, which is the reason Jim doesn't feel close to her now. He was brought up mostly by aunts."

"Why wasn't she around?" asked Maria.

"Well, it's a long story," said Anne, "And Jim probably wouldn't appreciate me repeating too much of it. But his mother was something of a feminist, before they'd invented the word. She was a journalist, and became a war correspondent. That's how she met Jim's dad . . . he was in the Army.

"When his father was killed, Bess went on working. I don't blame her in a way, because from what I understand she was a first class journalist . . . better than a lot of men. But in those days women were expected to stay home and mind their children, and Bess didn't go along with it. So naturally Jim resents the fact that other kids had their mothers around, and he didn't."

"What about now . . . is she still working?" asked Maria.

"No, she gave it up soon after we were married," said Anne. "She became interested in anthropology, and decided to do a University course. For the past eight years she's been traipsing around the Pacific. Every now and then she breezes in and breezes out again, or we get a postcard. Sometimes it's as long as a year without hearing a word. Don't ask me where she is right now . . . I wouldn't have a clue."

"She sounds interesting," said Maria. "I'd have thought Jim would be proud of her."

"Jim's proud of her professional achievements . . . but I think that deep down, he'd still rather have an ordinary, humdrum suburban mum like everyone else," said Anne. "It's made him very bitter . . . at times he feels she doesn't love him."

"I'm sure she does," said Maria. "In her own way. It's just that some people don't show it."

Anne agreed. "So you see why Jim doesn't want me to call the new baby Bess. He says if it's going to be called after a grandparent, then he'd rather it be Helen. And Helen won't hear of it . . . So that's that."

Dear Helen . . .

With the mention of her name, Maria remembered fondly the first time she'd met her. It was the day she and Max, with baby Shane, moved into Ramsay Street. Helen had been visiting the Robinsons, and had been outside watering the garden when the furniture van had pulled up. She had immediately smiled a welcome, and invited them both in for a cup of tea. Anne had been out shopping, and had called over later. But it was Helen who was the first friend Anne made in the street.

Later, when Maria was feeling rejected and lonely because of hurtful remarks about her "foreignness" and accent, Helen had encouraged her to join a community group for young mothers.

But the time when she had appreciated Helen's friendship most had been nearly eight years ago, when her marriage had been under severe strain. Helen had stepped in and cared for four-year-old Shane at her flat, to give Maria a chance to go away on her own and think things over.

And only Helen knew the real reason why Max resented Danny . . . a secret she and Maria shared together.

"Is it ready yet?"

Maria's reverie was interrupted by Julie putting her head around the door, and looking expectantly at her mother.

"Here comes Miss Impatience," laughed

Anne, looking around for a cake skewer, "All right, we'll give it a try. But if it sinks in the middle don't blame me."

It didn't sink, and the skewer came out almost clean. Anne told Julie to give it another five minutes, and they'd take it out. Julie could ice it, and maybe daddy would like some for his supper.

"I'd better be getting back," said Maria. "Glad you liked the nightie . . . take care of yourself." As she left, Jim passed her coming back from nextdoor.

Later that night in bed, with the house quiet and the children asleep, Jim told Anne about Ross Warner's proposal. Anne's immediate response was excitement. Why didn't he tell her the minute he came in through the door? And when would he start?

"Hey now, slow down to a gallop," said Jim. He hadn't expected Anne to show this much enthusiasm. She was usually the more cautious of the two, and never went into anything without first weighing all the pros and cons. It was a family joke often told and re-told by Helen that the only time in Anne's life she had ever taken an important step without pausing to think it through was when she'd said "yes" to Jim's marriage proposal.

Yet here she was almost urging Jim to accept

Ross Warner's offer.

"I'm not sure," said Jim. "I was keen at first, but now I've had a bit more time to think it through. What if the business flops? We could be right back where we started."

"We've been poor before, we can be poor again," said Anne, snuggling up to Jim and nuzzling into his neck. "Remember when we first got married . . . packing cases for furniture, and we slept on a mattress on the floor?"

"I hardly think it will come to that again," said Jim, smiling in the dark. "But it could be tough for a while. I don't like the idea of you having all the extra worry, as well as looking after a new baby. It's not fair on you."

Anne finally made Jim agree to a compromise suggestion. They'd invite Ross and his wife for dinner, and both hear him through. Then Jim could make the decision. And she wanted Jim to know that whatever he decided, she'd be behind him all the way.

"I love you," said Jim, as he leaned across and kissed Anne. Lying so close together, he could feel the movement of their unborn baby, stirring and kicking in the womb.

Not for the first time, Jim counted his blessings. If only everyone could be as happy as them . . .

Chapter 5

Helen checked her appearance in the mirror for the umpteenth time, and wondered again if she'd chosen the right dress. Was it too fussy? Should she change to the blue? It was the night of her dinner date with David Barrington, and already she was regretting that she'd accepted.

He seemed a nice man, and probably meant well. Two middleaged persons without partners . . . he probably thought he was being kind. At least it would be someone to talk to for an evening, instead of reading a book or watching TV.

But what if he asked her out again, and she didn't want to continue the acquaintance? Normally it wouldn't be a problem, she could always think up some tactful excuse. But the fact that they were also thrown together at the art class made it more complicated. They had to keep seeing each other, even if it was just side by side painting landscapes. It could be both embarrassing and awkward.

Helen was still debating whether she should change into the blue shirtdress, when the front door bell buzzed.

"It's me, David," she heard through the intercom.

Helen asked him to wait for her in the foyer, rather than come upstairs. Somehow it helped make it all a little more impersonal. She checked to make sure she'd turned off all the gas jets, switched on her hall light, and left the flat.

David was waiting at the glass security door when she arrived. He looked taller and heavier than she remembered him, and was rugged up with scarf and overcoat. He frowned when he saw she was wearing only a light jacket over her dress.

"It's cold outside," he said. "D'you want to go back and get something warmer?" It reminded her of Bill, he was always saying things like that, worrying whether she'd catch a chill.

Helen shook her head. David was right, it was almost wintry outside. Biut now that she was this far, she just wanted to press on and get the dinner over as quickly as good manners allowed. A drink or two, a meal, some conversation, coffee. At the very most, three hours. She had already decided when he took her home, she wouldn't invite him inside.

"I hope you'll like this place," said David, holding open the car door as they left the block of flats. "I used to eat there quite a bit when I was working fulltime . . . it's near my old office. It's changed hands since, but my colleagues tell me it's still good."

"I'm sure I'll like it,' said Helen. "Anything I haven't had to cook myself always tastes great to me."

"I know what you mean," said David, as they drove into the city. "My wife was a wonderful cook, I always used to say it was a waste of time going to eat because she could do it better. She enjoyed it . . . we used to have some wonderful dinner parties. When she went, I had to learn to fend for myself."

Wonderful cook . . . hostess . . . a woman of courage and vitality. Helen was beginning to build a picture of Janet Barrington in her mind. And it was clear the marriage had been a happy one.

"What kind of a cook are you now?" she asked.

"Would you believe that a few years ago, I couldn't even boil an egg?" said David. "I lived on takeaways. Then one night I was sitting with this bundle of fish and chips on my lap . . . I hadn't even taken it out of the paper and put it on a plate. And I suddenly thought, this is damn stupid. There can't be anything that hard about cooking a meal. So I bought some cookbooks, and practised a bit.''

"And . . .?" asked Helen, smiling.

"I still can't cook. Well, I can put together a rough meal of sorts . . . say, steak and chips. But that's about all.''

Helen laughed.

"So tonight has nothing to do with my charm and grace. It's just to save you from junk food,'' she said.

David grinned back at her.

"Something like that,'' he said. "But I like the charm and grace too. Well . . . here we are.''

The car had pulled up outside a building with no sign of a restaurant other than a printed menu in a glass case at the front. David helped Helen out, and they walked through swing doors to the rear. Tucked away from the noise of traffic, in a large room with beamed rafters and an open log fire, was the place where they would eat.

"I love a log fire,'' said Helen, as a waiter took her jacket and led them to their table.

"So do I,'' said David. "How about we have a drink in front of it, while we're working out what to eat?''

As they settled themselves by the fire, and studied the menu, Helen sneaked another look at David. For the painting classes he always wore casual clothes, a pair of sports trousers and sweater or shirt. But tonight he was neatly dressed in a dark grey suit and tie, his shirt immaculate, with a flash of gold cufflinks. Elegant, but not overdone. Helen liked a man who took pains with his appearance. She couldn't stand slobs.

David caught her looking, and smiled.

''Is it the tie or the cufflinks?'' he asked. ''The cufflinks were a present from Janet . . . I know they're not worn much these days, but she bought them for our wedding anniversary. The tie is for you — I decided to go out and splurge this afternoon.''

Helen felt herself going pink with embarrassment. Pull yourself together, she scolded. You're behaving like a simpering teenager.

''I didn't mean to stare,'' she said. ''It was rude of me.''

''Don't apologise . . . I'm flattered,'' said David. ''It isn't every day I get a chance to wine and dine a beautiful woman — and I warn you, I'm going to make the most of it. Now what'll we have to eat and drink?''

Helen ordered a gin and tonic, and David settled for scotch and soda. As she sipped her drink, and pondered what to eat, Helen felt her nervousness begin to slip away. Maybe it was the warmth of the log fire, or the relaxed atmosphere of the surroundings . . . or a bit of both. But Helen felt herself unwinding, and starting to enjoy the evening.

"D'you like lobster?" David was asking, as he studied the menu. "Personally, I'm more of a steak man . . . but I know the lobster is very good here."

It had been years since Helen had eaten lobster. Usually, when she went to restaurants, she settled for something more modest in price. Not that she didn't indulge herself now and then, but on the small income left by Bill she had to watch the budget. When she ate out, either on her own or with friends, she usually looked for inexpensive places that served simple, no-nonsense meals. Nothing fussy. And definitely nothing in the lobster class.

"I'll have it," decided Helen. "How about you?"

David opted for the carpetbag steak, and talked Helen into an unusual entree of baked avocado with prawns and bacon. That done, he settled himself back in his chair and raised his glass in a toast.

"To us," he said. "To a happy evening."

The evening went so fast, that Helen was surprised later to look at her watch and find it already ten o'clock.

She told David more about her early marriage, the financial struggles, and how she felt when doctors told her after the birth of Anne that she could have no more babies.

"I was devastated," said Helen. "I cried for days. I was still in my teens, and I couldn't believe this was the end of it all. So I know how your wife felt. It's a terrible thing for a woman."

"It was pretty rough on Janet too," admitted David. "She lost a couple, before they finally told her it was hopeless. By the time we got around to thinking of adoption, we were too old. And I'm not sure I wanted it, anyway. I know it's the wrong way to look at it, but I wasn't keen on bringing up another man's child."

Helen hesitated, as though about to speak, and David picked up on the look on her face.

"Did I say something?" he asked.

"I adopted," said Helen.

"But you had a child," said David.

"I know, but neither of us wanted her to grow up lonely. We'd both come from largish families — three girls, in my case, and Bill had brothers. Only children can become selfish, and

48

we didn't want that for Anne. So we put our names down for adoption.

"What we didn't realise was how long it would take. Everyone wanted babies, and the fact that we already had one went against us. Finally we heard of one through a private agency, and got a beautiful little girl. But it took us five years."

"Where is she now?" asked David.

"She's in the States at the moment, somewhere on the West coast. I had a letter from her the other day, and she's thinking of staying on and working," said Helen. She pulled out a snapshot from her handbag. It showed Helen with her two daughters . . . Anne small, dark-haired, smiling. And Rosemary, a striking-looking, glamorous blonde.

"She could be a model," commented David, handing back the snapshots. "Or a movie actress. She certainly has the looks for it."

"Looks are deceptive," said Helen. "Rosemary isn't interested in a glamour career. She's a very clever girl, graduated Honours from University. She knows more about finance and business than most men her age."

"Sounds like you have a pretty interesting family," said David.

"I have," agreed Helen. "You must meet them some time."

The words were out of her mouth almost without her thinking. David seized on it instantly, and said he would enjoy it. Since Janet died, he didn't go out much any more. Most of his friends were married, and his only relatives lived interstate.

"I'm a social embarrassment," he said, smiling. "The odd one out at dinner parties. The world is made for couples, I've found out. Or if they invite me, then they sit me next to some husband-hunting merry widow."

He stopped, embarrassed, as he realised what he'd said.

Helen laughed. "Don't worry, it's the same for me," she said. "Except all my friends have given up on me by now. They've stopped trying to match me up with eligible gentlemen. The last eligible gentleman they trotted out was 69, with a hearing problem."

David laughed with her, and poured them another glass of wine.

Helen was amazed at how much she was enjoying the evening, and how easy she found it to talk to David. He mentioned his wife again only briefly, taking out a snapshot from his wallet. He apologised for his wife's gaunt appearance, saying the photo had been taken in the last year of her illness.

"She was beautiful when she was younger,"

he said. "Watching someone you love die, bit by bit, is a terrible experience. You're lucky that your husband went quickly."

They passed on to other things, and Helen discovered they both liked whodunnits. They also shared a love of the same music, and David mentioned a concert coming up next Thursday. Would Helen care to go with him? Helen would, but unfortunately had a prior commitment. A meeting of the local Community Council, which she'd offered to chair.

It was almost eleven when David delivered her home. He didn't ask to come in, and Helen stuck to her promise and didn't offer a nightcap.

"When will I see you again?" he asked, as Helen fished for her key at the front door.

"At the art class," said Helen lightly, knowing that wasn't what David meant. But she was deliberately trying to keep it impersonal.

"Thanks for a wonderful evening," said Helen, holding out her hand. "I really enjoyed it."

David ignored the hand. Instead, he leaned down and kissed her. It wasn't a passionate kiss, but it was more than just a friendly gesture. Then he walked back to his car.

Back in the safety of her small flat, Helen leaned against her front door. She could still feel David's kiss tingling on her lips. And she knew he would ask her out again.

Should she nip it in the bud right now, before it developed into anything more serious? Or accept, and see what happened. Helen felt attracted to him, and knew it was mutual. But she had been a widow now for six years, and had developed her own special way of life. It was selfish, she knew, but she enjoyed her independence. She liked having to only answer to herself, to retreat into silence with a book or music if she didn't feel like talking to anyone. She had loved Bill deeply, but those last years before he died had been very demanding.

Finally Helen decided that if David asked her out again, she would accept. They had similar interests, enjoyed the same things, and were both sensible enough not to get carried away by it all. It would be a pleasant friendship, based on mutual loneliness.

And after all, what harm could it do?

Chapter 6

Ross Warner arrived precisely on time, with his wife Margaret. She was a pleasant fair-haired woman in her early to mid thirties, dressed in a conservative skirt and twinset. Jim was a bit surprised at Ross' choice of wife — at University, he had always gone for the flashy types, the head-turners. She looked precisely what Ross had said she was, a company secretary. But they seemed very happy together.

Jim took their coats, and ushered them into the living room. He explained Anne was with the children, but would join them in a moment.

"I understand from Ross you're expecting another," said Margaret, bringing out a small gift-wrapped package. "It's not much, but I couldn't resist it."

Anne came into the room, and Jim introduced her. She opened the package, to find an exquisitely embroidered matinee jacket.

"It's Swiss," explained Margaret. "Hand

53

made . . . I thought it might be a bit different from the usual thing. Although I suppose with four, you've got heaps of clothes.''

"Nothing like this," said Anne, holding it up and showing it to Jim. "It's beautiful, almost too good to use. I love it!"

Jim poured drinks, and they sat in the living room catching up on the past years. Or rather, Jim and Ross talked, and the two wives listened. Anne had the feeling that Margaret was a shade uncomfortable, not quite at her ease. Ross, on the other hand, was all joviality and good humour.

"How about this fellow of yours?" he said to Anne, slapping Jim on the back. "Eleven years, and he hasn't changed a bit. I would've known him anywhere.''

Jim grinned, and poured Ross another drink.

"Clean living," he said. "My family keep me young.''

"Say, d'you remember Goulash?" asked Ross. "That lecturer everyone hated, the one with the thick accent. Nobody could understand what he was saying half the time. Well, I ran into him the other day. He's now a professor at some tinpot college in the States, one of those places no one's ever heard of. He was out here on a sabbatical.''

Jim remembered the lecturer Ross was talking about. He had been a refugee from the Hungarian uprising of 1956, and had a Doctorate of Philosophy from the University of Budapest. But because of his problems coping with English, and the fact that he had fled his country leaving behind his academic records, he had been reduced to lecturing first year students. They had been a cruel lot, Jim remembred, mimicking his accent and at one time letting off a stink bomb in the lecture theatre. No one had owned up to the bomb, and Goulash had finally walked out of the theatre, redfaced and angry, swearing never to come back. But he had, forced back by the need to earn a living.

It had seemed just a lot of fun at the time, harmless student pranks against an unpopular lecturer. But looking back, Jim now realised what agony of spirit they had probably put him through.

"I don't remember you mentioning him," said Anne, leading the way into the dining room. "Was he the one who failed you in first year physics?"

"That's the one," said Jim. "He failed half the class. "But we demanded a re-mark, and most of us managed to scrape through. I'd almost forgotten about it."

"It was the only time your husband here ever did badly in anything," said Ross. "I hope you realise what a brain you married . . . Jim was the star student — the one who was going places.''

Jim wondered, as they sat down at the table, if that was meant to be a subtle swipe at the fact he hadn't managed to go any place except a safe job in a Government department. He knew, from the glance Anne exchanged with him, that she was thinking the same thing.

There was no more talk about University or Jim's job prospects for the remainder of the dinner. Instead, they talked about inconsequential things such as movies, the weather, children, the best kind of car to drive, and holidays. Ross said he and Margaret planned to go to Bali next year. Jim had to admit that with the new baby coming, they'd be lucky if they could afford more than a week at a caravan park.

Anne had gone to special pains with this dinner, and both Ross and Margaret complimented her on it. Mushroom shrimp bisque, one of Anne's specialties, followed by rack of lamb and then apple pie. Anne was famous for her apple pies, light and flaky packed with apple and brown sugar. She'd been taught well by Helen. Ross had a second serve, commenting ''to hell with the waistline.''

It wasn't until coffee that Ross raised the reason for him being there. He told Anne that he knew she probably had a few misgivings, but there was no one he'd rather work with than Jim Robinson. It was a waste of talent for Jim to be locked away in a department where his brains weren't appreciated. If they went into partnership together, then it would be a case of the sky's the limit. They could go as far as they wanted, instead of waiting around for people to die or retire.

Ross outlined his proposal. He'd already found suitable premises, and had an option on a longterm lease. He would run the business and marketing side, while Jim took charge of ideas and development. They'd both take a minimum salary for the first year, and plough all the profits back into the company. By the second or third year, they should be successfully established. From then on, it would just be a matter of consolidate and expand.

Ross Warner's enthusiasm began to rub off on Jim and Anne. Ross told Anne, smilingly, that when she got tired of changing nappies she could take a turn working in the office. They'd need some staff, and it would keep it in the family. Besides, said Ross, it was good for a wife to have an outside interest. He didn't believe in all that baloney about a woman's place only being in the bedroom and the kitchen. Look at Margaret here, she'd still kept on with her job.

Anne, with a quick glance at Jim, said she thought she'd leave that kind of thing to others. She had nothing against wives working, but she'd never been a career person. She didn't feel trapped, she enjoyed looking after Jim and the children.

"Please yourself," said Ross jovially. "Just thought I'd mention it, that's all. So what's the decision?"

Jim looked at Anne, who nodded.

"Count me in," he said. "I'll do it."

Ross jumped to his feet, and held out his hand to Jim.

"Shake, partner," he said. "You'll never regret this."

Jim remembered a bottle of champagne he'd put aside for the baby's christening, and brought it out so they could celebrate. They toasted each other, and the new business. There was some discussion about names — should it be Warner and Robinson, or Robinson and Warner? They decided to defer it until the business was registered. Maybe it should be something impersonal, using neither of their names.

Then as they were celebrating, Ross dropped the bombshell.

"By the way, we'll need some capital," he said. "I've got about $20,000 put aside. I assume you want to go into this on an equal basis.

Can you put your hands on the same amount?"

Jim was so shocked, he couldn't give an immediate answer. Instead, he made some noncommittal remark, and changed the subject.

Later that night, in bed, Jim and Anne discussed Ross Warner's proposal. Jim now felt inclined to turn it down — to raise that kind of money, he would have to mortgage the house. And he didn't feel he should commit himself to such a debt, with a new baby coming. It was too much of a gamble.

But Anne wasn't so sure. She'd been fired by Ross' enthusiasm, and she knew Jim liked the idea of being his own boss. This might be the only chance he would get.

"I can't do it," said Jim. "It isn't fair on you. We'll be in debt up to our eyes, it will take us years to get on top."

Anne pulled herself up on one elbow, and looked down at Jim. She could feel the baby kicking and stirring, and her back was starting to ache.

"We've always been honest with each other," she said. "Just tell me one thing . . . would you like to do it?"

Jim hesitated a moment, then answered truthfully.

"I would," he said.

"Then do it," said Anne. "Mortgage the

house. We've got some savings, let's put it all into the business. We've been poor before, and it won't hurt to be poor again. We'll manage somehow. In fact, it could be fun . . . just like when we were first married. And it's not as though it's going to be forever. Once you get started, you'll soon be making money. Please, Jim, you've got to do it . . . you mightn't get this chance again."

Jim looked at Anne, and kissed her.

"I love you," he said.

"That isn't an answer," replied Anne. "Tell me you'll take it on . . . please."

Jim pulled Anne close to him. Not for the first time, he marvelled at his luck in finding such a perfect woman. Anne was more than a wife and lover, she was also his closest friend.

"If you believe in me so much," said Jim, "I'll do it!"

It would be hard, certainly and mean a lot of sacrifice. They would need to budget carefully, and go without a lot of things. No more holidays, no new clothes for the two of them. The building of the new room would have to be postponed, and also Jim's plans for repainting and upgrading the house.

The repayments on the mortgage would take every bit of spare money they had.

But they were both still young, and the possibilities were endless and exciting. Warner and Robinson . . . Robinson and Warner. And who knows? Maybe sometime it could even be Robinson and Sons.

Jim fell asleep, his arms around Anne, dreaming of a rosy future.

Chapter 7

"G RAN . . . Gran!!" As soon as Helen walked through the door, the three Robinson children hurled themselves at her.

It was Saturday morning, and Helen had come for the weekend . . . partly to see her family, but also to give Anne some help. Although Anne had always sailed through her pregnancies ("a natural mother", her doctor used to say), this was a time when strain and tiredness took over. Having Helen in the house meant that Anne could put her feet up, take a rest, and also enjoy the luxury of someone else cooking a meal.

For her part, Helen looked forward to seeing her grandchildren, hearing the latest news from school, and sharing in their lives.

She was a loving grandmother, kind but still firm, and a visit from Grandma Daniels was always something special. They clustered around, as she opened her overnight bag and took out small gifts for them all — a sports magazine for Paul, jigsaw puzzle for Scott, and some hair ribbons for Julie.

"You spoil them," said Anne, smiling, as she came over and kissed her mother.

"I haven't anyone else to spoil," Helen smiled back. "How're you feeling?"

"Not bad," said Anne. "But I'm getting a lot of backache. Also cramps in my legs. Jim thinks this one's going to be a boy."

Helen looked at her daughter, concerned. Although Anne was never one to complain, Helen felt she was looking more strained and tired than usual. She was pale, with dark shadows under her eyes and looked as though she hadn't been getting a lot of sleep.

"You're on your feet too much," said Helen. "Just as well I came over . . . now sit down, that's an order. The children can take my bag to my room. I'm going to make us a cup of tea."

Anne didn't need much persuasion to sit down. This baby was very active, much more uncomfortable than the other ones had been, and she was finding it hard to relax. Whoever said it got easier each time, was definitely not a mother.

Anne lay back and closed her eyes. It was nice to be fussed over, like when she was a small girl. She could still remember the time she and Rosemary both had measles, and Helen had pushed their beds together. Then she'd read them stories, and cooked all their favourite foods. Anne wondered where Rosemary was now. Although they were very different, the two sisters had always been close. Anne missed having Rosemary around. She was a fun person, and lit up a room when she walked into it. All the children loved Aunt Rosemary.

Maybe she'd meet someone while she was in the States. Rosemary had always said she wasn't interested in marriage, but Anne was sure it was only because the right person hadn't come along. She'd like to see Rosemary settle down, and be as happy as she was. But Rosemary was choosy about her men . . . and then again, husbands like Jim were a bit thin on the ground.

Jim . . . so kind and loving and thoughtful. And now this big opportunity that had been dropped into his lap.

Anne was still thinking about Jim, when Helen came back with two cups of tea.

"Penny for them," she said, as she sat down on the sofa alongside Anne.

"I was thinking how wonderful it's going to be when Jim and Ross get started," said Anne. She and Jim had already told Helen about the move, and Helen had given the scheme her whole-hearted approval. "Go for it," she'd said on the phone. "I think it's terrific."

Jim walked in right at that moment. He greeted his mother-in-law warmly, then reminded Anne this was the day of the beach picnic. Max was already loading up the van, and Maria had prepared enough food for the two families. She wasn't going herself, as she had to visit a friend in hospital. But there was plenty of room for both Anne and Helen.

Anne begged off, saying she didn't feel up to coping with a picnic. And Helen decided to stay home and keep her company.

"You all right?" asked Jim anxiously, noting that Anne looked a bit pale.

"I'm fine," said Anne. "It's purely vanity. I don't fancy sitting around a beach looking like this, with all those slim young things running around in bikinis. You and Max go, the kids'll enjoy it. And thank Maria for the food."

When they'd gone, Helen took out some knitting. It was the baby shawl, still only half finished.

"I meant to have this ready for you by the weekend," Helen said. "Blame David for it."

Anne raised an eyebrow. David who? Helen explained he was a fellow student from her painting class, and they'd been out to dinner together.

"And don't look at me like that," she added. "There's absolutely nothing in it . . . we're just friends."

"I didn't say anything," smiled Anne. "But I'm glad you've met someone nice. Are you going to bring him around so we can inspect him?"

"Absolutely not," said Helen. "I know what you and Jim are like, you couple of match-makers. Anyway we've only been out once . . . he probably won't ask me again."

"I bet he will," said Anne, teasing. "You're not a bad catch for a Merry Widow, y'know . . . good figure, nice hair, nice eyes, intelligent, charming . . ."

". . . and very happy single, thank you," said Helen, tossing a cushion at her daughter.

They went off to Anne's bedroom to inspect some of the baby things, including the Swiss matinee jacket Margaret Warner had brought around the other night.

"How're things going with the new business?" asked Helen.

"Couldn't be better," said Anne. "I haven't seen Jim so excited in years, he's just like a kid with a new toy. He's either on the phone talking to Ross, or he's sitting at the kitchen table working out new projects. I'm lucky if I get two words out of him. You know he's resigned his job?"

"I didn't, but I was expecting it," said Helen. "How did they take it?"

"Very well," said Anne. "His boss was particularly nice, and said if he ever changed his mind they'd welcome him back again. But he won't, of course. You know Jim . . . once he has his heart set on something, there's no stopping him. This is the biggest chance of his life, and he's determined to make it succeed."

"And how about you?" asked Helen anxiously. "You're looking a bit tired, y'know. Would you like me to move in early, and give you a hand?"

Anne thanked her for the offer, but declined. "I'll manage," she said "and the kids are very good. There'll be plenty for you to do once the baby comes."

*   *   *

At the picnic, Danny and Scott were making sand castles. Julie, who had refused to get into her swimsuit because she said it was too cold, had hitched up her dress and was paddling in the shallows looking for jellyfish. Shane and Paul were having races along the beach.

"Look at him," said Max admiringly, as he

watched Shane streak ahead of Paul. "A natural athlete. Reminds me of myself at the same age."

"Yeah, you weren't bad," Jim remembered. "How's Shane going with his training?"

"A little beauty," said Max with pride. "He did a high dive the other day, you wouldn't believe. Did I tell you I'm thinking of putting in a pool?"

"No," said Jim. "But it's a good idea, you've got room for it."

Jim wasn't surprised at Max's decision. Every time they went to the beach, Max complained about the distance they had to travel, the traffic jams, the problems of trying to find a decent parking space. Today it had taken them an hour to get there. When they finally arrived, Max's mood wasn't improved by finding that their favourite picnic spot had been taken, and they'd had to move further along the beach.

"Sunday drivers," growled Max, as a car cut in on him. "Think they own the flamin' road."

"What's it going to cost?" asked Jim.

"Dunno. I'm getting a mate of mine to put together a few estimates next week," said Max. "Thought I might do some of the work myself, then sub-contract. How'd you feel about giving me a hand with the design?"

"Anytime," said Jim. "I'll come over tomorrow and take some measurements.''

Danny and Scott rushed up, and said they were starving. How about some food? Max opened the hamper Maria had prepared, and handed out sandwiches. Danny inspected his, and his face fell.

"I don't like tomato, can I change?'' he asked.

"Eat what you're given,'' said Max. Jim noticed his voice was unusually sharp.

Danny tried again. "There's plenty, can I swap for a cheese?'' Max's face darkened.

"No, now buzz off,'' he said. "Stop pestering me.'' Danny went back to his sand castles with Scott, looking annoyed.

"That kid does what he wants,'' said Max to Jim. "Trouble is, Maria spoils him. She lets him get away with it.'' Jim privately thought it was a lot of fuss to make about a tomato sandwich, but sensing Max's mood, said nothing. Instead, he started asking more about the swimming pool Max planned to build — where exactly did he think of putting it?

Max drew a rough outline in the sand, showing where it would be in relation to the house.

"Why don't you put one in yourself?'' he asked Jim. "You do the engineering work, I'll throw in the plumbing. We do it together, we can cut costs.''

Jim shook his head.

"Sorry, Max," he said. "But I've got a few other things on my plate right now. I can't afford it. Maybe in a few years. But it's a nice thought, thanks for the offer."

*　　*　　*

Later that night in bed, Jim told Anne about Max's swimming pool plans.

"You know why he's doing it," he said. "It's all for Shane. If he can make that boy a champion, Max'll die happy."

"D'you think he's pushing him too much?" asked Anne. "Maria was talking to me about it the other day. She's worried Shane will burn out before he has a chance to do anything. I wouldn't like to put one of our children through anything like that . . . even if they had the talent."

"Which they haven't," said Jim, ruffling her hair. "Thank goodness we've got nice, ordinary kids."

"That's because they've got nice, ordinary parents," said Anne. "Anyway, enough about Max and his swimming pool . . . I've got something far more interesting to tell you. Guess what, Mum has a beau!"

Anne told Jim about Helen's dinner date with David Barrington, and they discussed the possibilities. Jim was as intrigued as Anne, because it was the first time either had heard Helen mention another man. And Anne's imagination was working overtime, building David as a possible suitor.

"Hey, slow down," said Jim eventually. "She's only been out with him once. There may be nothing in it."

"But you must admit it would be nice if there were," said Anne. "After all, it's been six years now since Dad died. She must get lonely at times."

It was finally decided to see if Helen would bring her new friend around for dinner one night, to give Jim and Anne a chance to inspect him.

"I'll do it so she won't suspect," said Anne. "Something subtle."

Jim grinned in the darkness, and hugged Anne to him.

"I know you," he said. "It'll be about as subtle as a sledge-hammer. Helen will catch on immediately. But I like the idea of having him over. My mother-in-law's very special, and I want to make sure this David bloke is good enough for her."

"Now who's match making?" asked Anne.

71

"Right I'll ask her tomorrow."

She curled up and went to sleep dreaming of babies, romance, and wedding bells.

Chapter 8

O N the Monday, Jim took the step that sealed
his future. He went to the local branch of
the Pacific Bank, and signed the papers for the
loan on his house. Then he rang Ross Warner
and told him to go ahead and draw up the partnership agreement.

"This calls for a celebration," said Ross.
"Margaret's tied up all day, but I'm in the clear.
Why don't you bring Anne into town, and we'll
all have lunch together?"

Jim had been planning to take Anne to lunch
himself. It was her 31st birthday, and with a
new baby about to be born this one was doubly
important. It might be the last chance for some
time that he and Anne could go out to a restaurant together, just the two of them. But when
he mentioned it to Anne she was insistent he accept Ross Warner's offer. Her birthday could
wait.

So they met Ross at his city club, and toasted

the new business partnership with champagne.

Jim noted the champagne was French imported. He demurred at the extravagance, and also offered to pay for his share of the lunch. But Ross wouldn't hear of it, especially when he found out it was Anne's birthday.

"Plenty of time for that when we get going," he said. "This is on me, just to say how delighted I am that we'll be working together." He raised his glass in a toast. "Here's to our first million."

Jim grinned. Ross had always been the super optimist when he was at University, the one with the grandiose get-rich-quick schemes. And he hadn't changed.

Jim raised his glass also, and touched Anne's. "To us," he said.

After lunch, Ross drove them out to look at the site for the new engineering plant. Jim had already inspected it, but Ross wanted Anne to see it.

The workshop and offices were not far from Erinsborough, in an outlying suburb that was zoned light industrial. The premises weren't large, but the building was modern with room on both sides to expand. They had taken out an initial lease for five years, with an option to buy.

As they walked through it, Ross explained to

Anne the functions of the various areas.

"This will be Jim's office," he said. "We tossed a coin, and Jim won the room with the view. But he'll probably be spending most of his time out in the workshop. I'm planning to work the guts out of this guy of yours."

Anne liked Jim's office. It was large and airy, with plenty of room for his drawing table and desk. A window looked out on grass and trees.

Anne made a mental note to buy him an electric jug, so he could make tea or coffee whenever he wanted. At his old job, there had been a tea lady, Mabel, who used to wheel around the trolley twice a day and pass on the office gossip. Jim had a soft spot for her — and he'd told Anne he didn't mind leaving his colleagues behind, but he'd miss Mabel.

"So what d'you think, Anne?" asked Ross.

"I think it's wonderful," Anne answered. "What's the business going to be called?"

Ross glanced at Jim. "Well, we've tossed around a few, but we haven't come up with the right one yet. Any ideas?"

"None," said Anne. "I'll leave that kind of thing to you two business brains."

They walked back to the car, and Ross offered to drop them in the city. Jim had parked his own car near the club, and wanted to go back to his old office to collect a few personal things from a locker. Anne said she might take the opportunity to do some shopping. One of the stores was having a sale, and she needed some school clothes for Julie.

"Want me to pick you up somewhere when you've finished?" asked Jim, as he got back into his car. Anne thanked him, but said she'd take the bus home. She knew what would happen once he went back to the office. There would be friends wanting to hear about his new venture. Yarning with his old workmates could take hours.

Besides, it was almost three, and the children would soon be home from school. They all had keys, even young Scott, and could let themselves into the hosue if no one was home. But Anne was an oldfashioned mother, and liked to be there when they hurtled through the door calling out the latest news. For Anne, it was the best time of the day. Working mums missed a lot.

*   *   *

That night, the Robinsons had a double celebration — Jim's new business, and Anne's birthday.

Jim and Anne called the children together,

and announced the news that Jim had resigned his job and would be starting out on his own.

"Does that mean we're rich?" asked Julie.

"Not yet," said Jim, smiling. "It means we're going to be poor for a while. No more holidays away, no expensive Christmas presents. Everyone will have to do without and tighten the belt, until I can get the business on its feet."

Paul immediately offered to do a paper run, and Scott told Jim he could have the money in his piggy bank. Jim said he didn't think it would come to that yet. But he was pleased at how well the children were co-operating. Even Julie, who loved new clothes, said she supposed she could do without for a while.

Helen came over for dinner, and brought Anne the baby shawl she'd just finished. She also had something else, a large cardboard box. When Anne opened it, she took out a dress . . . her favourite color, blue sprigged with tiny flowers.

"If it doesn't fit when you have the baby, I can change it," said Helen. "But I wanted you to have something new when you come home from hospital. And I know you and Jim are watching your pennies right now."

"It's beautiful," said Anne, holding it up in front of her. "I'll make it fit, even if I have to exercise every day. What d'you think, darling?"

She looked at Jim.

"I think it will go perfectly with what I've bought you," he said.

He pulled out a small jewel box, and handed it over. "I was going to save this for later, but you might as well have it now."

Anne opened the jewel box, and gasped when she saw what was inside. On a white satin lining was an exquisitely fine gold chain and cross. It was a replica of one Jim had given her when they were married, which she'd later lost. Jim had said then that he'd buy her another one, but she'd talked him out of it, reminding him he was still a struggling University student. Then when their finances had improved, she'd forgotten about it. She thought Jim had, too . . . until today.

"It's too much," she said, as Jim took the chain from the box and fastened it around her neck. "I told you to forget about a birthday present this year . . . remember, you're out of work. You said yourself, we have to budget."

"Time enough for that later," said Jim, snapping the chain into place. "This is my one last extravagance. And this time, don't lose it."

The children all clustered around and admired the necklet. Then they produced their own gifts. Birthdays were big events in the Robinson family, and were always observed in the traditional way.

Paul had bought his mother a fun apron, printed with the words: STAY OUT OF MY WAY WHEN I'M COOKING. Julie's gift was something she'd made herself, an embroidered hand towel. And Scott, with some help from Jim, had come up with Anne's favourite bath talc. Each of the gifts was carefully wrapped, with little handwritten notes. Scott's had on it: I LOVE YOU, MUMMY in his seven-year-old scrawl. Anne felt tears sting her eyes as she unwrapped each one, and looked at the loving faces around her.

"I love you, too," she said to Scott, as she read his note, and put it with the rest of her presents. She gave him a big hug and kiss. Although Anne loved all of her children, her last-born was that bit more special. Soon, he wouldn't be the baby any more. A new little Robinson would take his place as the youngest in the family.

After the unwrapping of the presents, the birthday cake was brought out. Maria had made it, and brought it over earlier with some flowers from the Ramsay family. There were 31 candles on the cake, and Jim had some trouble lighting all of them.

"Next year, you'd better go back to being a teenager," he teased Anne, as yet another candle blew out before he could light the next one.

The 31 were finally lit, and Anne blew them out with some help from Scott and Julie.

"Make a wish, make a wish," chorused the children.

"I wish we could always be as happy as we are today," said Anne, her eyes closed.

"You're not supposed to tell," said Paul. "That means you won't get it."

Helen started to clear the dishes, as they all got up from the dining table.

"You go along and put your feet up," she said to Anne. "Julie and I can look after these."

Anne followed Jim and the boys into the living room without a protest. To tell the truth, she was beginning to feel tired. All the excitement of the day, the lunch in town, the trip to inspect the new engineering plant, were beginning to catch up with her.

When Helen and Julie rejoined them, the family photo albums came out — another Robinson birthday tradition. Although they'd done it before, the children always loved looking at pictures of themselves when very young. There was one of Paul as a baby, held in Anne's arms. And another of Jim and Anne on their wedding day.

"See, there's the gold cross," Anne pointed out. It had been a very small and simple wedding, but she'd worn the traditional white gown. The gift that Jim had given her could clearly be seen, around her neck.

At nine, Julie and Paul went off to their rooms to finish their homework, while young Scott was packed off to bed. Helen, Anne and Jim lingered over another coffee, still looking at the photo album.

"I can't believe I was ever as young as that," said Anne, turning back to the photo of her with baby Paul. "And look at that awful dress I'm wearing."

Helen reminded Anne that she, too, had been a wife and mother at the same age.

"A couple of child brides," teased Jim, with an affectionate grin at his two favourite women.

Mention of Helen's own marriage prompted Anne to bring up the question of asking David Barrington to dinner. She tried to make the invitation as casual as she could, but as Jim had predicted, Helen was immediately suspicious.

"Are you trying to marry me off?" she demanded. Her tone was fierce, but her eyes were smiling.

Anne protested nothing was further from her mind. No, all she wanted was to meet Helen's new friend from her painting class. Helen had mentioned he was an accountant. Maybe he

81

could be of some help to Jim in the new business.

"Keep me out of it," said Jim, throwing up his arms. Helen finally agreed she would see if David were free one night, during the coming week. But she warned Anne — not one word that would even suggest the relationship was anything more serious than just a casual acquaintance.

"He's just a friend," she told her daughter. "We like each other's company, that's all. It's not going to lead to anything."

And by this time, Helen had convinced even herself of the truth of what she was saying. David had asked her out as an act of kindness, nothing more. Other than meeting at the art class, she probably wouldn't hear from him again.

Chapter 9

THE phone was ringing in Helen's flat as she turned the key in the door, on her return from the Robinsons. As she picked up the receiver, she knew instinctively who it was.

"Hello there," said David. "I've been trying to get you all evening. Where've you been?"

Helen explained about the birthday dinner, and passed on Anne's invitation. David accepted, and they settled on next Friday. He told her the reason he was ringing . . . a friend of his, with a concert subscription, had gone away and given David his tickets. Would Helen care to come with him tomorrow?

This time Helen didn't hesitate before she accepted. She knew the soloist by reputation, a Czech-born violinist, and had wanted to hear him. And by now she'd convinced herself there could be no harm in continuing to see David.

"Good, I'll pick you up at six," said David. "We'll eat somewhere first." He'd put down

the phone, before Helen could do anything
about the dinner date. But again, she didn't
worry.

Two dinners and a concert don't add up to a
serious relationship. Besides, she found herself
looking forward to seeing him again. He was the
only person she knew who shared her passion
for art and classical music. Bill had enjoyed
going to the occasional concert, but his music
tastes leaned more towards Mantovani and
Sinatra. And he'd never been keen on being
dragged through an art gallery.

Helen had acquired her love for art while at
boarding school. Art had been a compulsory
subject, even in that provincial country town in
Queensland. The principal was an unmarried
Englishwoman, Miss Spiers. She was a highly
educated woman, elegant and cultured.
Rumour among the students was that she'd fled
to Australia after a broken love affair, but no
one ever knew the truth of it. She never spoke
of her family, although again it was rumoured
they were highborn and titled. One of Helen's
classmates swore she'd seen a letter arrive with
a ducal crest on it.

Whatever the reason for her coming to Australia, and burying herself in a remote
Queensland town, she was determined to instill
in her colonial 'gels' a knowledge and love of

the best of European culture.

For most of them, daughters of sheep farmers and country shopkeepers, it was just something to be endured until they could escape to marriage or jobs in the big city. But Helen had been one of the ones on whom the fiery enthusiasm of Miss Spiers had rubbed off. If she had stayed on longer, and not married Bill so young, she would like to have become an art teacher.

Next morning, Helen made an appointment to have her hair done. Then she went through her wardrobe, taking a lot of time to choose the right dress. She finally settled on a pale pink chiffon, one she'd bought last time Rosemary had been in Australia. Rosemary had liked it, and told Helen it made her look 10 years younger. Helen had worried a bit about it, wondering if it made her look like mutton dressed up as lamb. But Rosemary had insisted, and even told the salesgirl to charge it to her. Helen had been saving it for the christening of Anne and Jim's baby, but decided a concert might be the right time to bring it out again. She looked at herself critically, as she tried it on in front of a mirror. Did it really make her look younger? She was lucky that she wasn't one of those women who put on weight as they got older — she was almost exactly the same size, as she had been at twenty. Fair hair, with just a hint of silvery grey to it. Blue eyes. A few laughter lines at the eyes and mouth, but otherwise not too bad. Good legs. She'd always been lucky with her legs. Bill used to say jokingly they were the reason he fell for her.

Stop thinking about Bill.

Think instead about tonight's meeting, and what they'd talk about. Helen decided this time she'd stick to impersonal subjects.

No more talk about lost spouses, loneliness, or love. No baring of souls, no intimate secrets. Instead, she'd stick to mundane family things like Jim's new business, or art and music. Safe topics, that wouldn't draw her into dangerous territory.

The front buzzer sounded promptly at six, and Helen went down to meet David. He was immediately admiring of her dress, telling her she looked beautiful. "You should always wear pink," he said. "It suits you."

They went to the same restaurant where they'd eaten before, and again sat in front of the roaring log fire. This time Helen had heeded the weather signals, and had worn a short fur jacket over her dress. As David leaned over, to help her off with it, she felt an unexpected stirring of excitement, a feeling she hadn't experienced for years. Just as quickly she shrugged it off, and started telling him about Anne's birthday dinner and her son-in-law's new plans for the future.

"It's going to be hard for them," she said. "Three young children, and another one on the way. I told Jim you might be able to give him some advice on the business side."

"I'd be glad to," said David. "A couple of my clients have done the same thing as Jim, gone into business for themselves. There are a few pitfalls, but from what you tell me he seems a level-headed, sensible sort of bloke. I'm looking forward to meeting him. And the rest of the family."

Again, a feeling of unease. Had she been unwise to go along with Anne, and invite David to dinner with the Robinsons? It had seemed harmless at the time, but maybe he was reading more into it than she intended. That mention of meeting the family. Somehow it had a feeling of intimacy.

Helen kept the conversation lighthearted and casual, as they had their pre-dinner drinks and then moved to their table.

Then they went on to the concert, and David took her home again. At the door, she neatly avoided another goodnight kiss, putting out her hand to shake his, and thanking him for a wonderful time.

David looked puzzled, but made no comment

. . . beyond reminding her they had an art class together in the morning. He'd pick her up, and they'd go together. Helen protested she could walk, as she always did, but David insisted. She finally decided to keep protesting seemed ungracious, and also made her sound like a bit of a fool.

"Thanks, that would be very nice," said Helen, and went through the security doors.

As she was about to get into the elevator she looked back, and saw David still standing there, watching her. She gave him a wave, as she disappeared inside.

In her flat, Helen switched on the light and noticed she'd left one of her paintings propped against the bookcase. It was the one of Anne in the garden, the painting that David had admired.

She decided she was too restless to go to bed right now, she'd do a bit more work on it. Helen hung up the pink dress, and changed into her painting smock. Then she put the picture on an easel, and took out her brushes.

Yes, it was a nice picture, she decided . . . looking at it thoughtfully. A happy picture, full of sunshine and joy. And Anne, although her features were too small to be recognisable, seemed to be part of the happiness, clutching the armful of daffodils close to her. With the sun behind her head, she had about her a glow that was almost an aura.

Helen picked up one of the brushes, and with a few deft movements began painting.

*   *   *

The students filed into their places at the art class, and set up their easels ready for work. David had been late picking up Helen, due to some trouble with his car. He'd turned up, breathless and apologetic, just as Helen was looking at her watch and beginning to think she'd have to walk.

They were the last two students to arrive, just as Lawrence Manning walked into the large, airy studio.

"Attention, ladies and gentlemen," he said, tapping his stick on the wooden floor. "Before we start today's class, I have something to announce."

"Due to an unexpected cancellation, one of our galleries has some dates free for a showing. The gallery director is a personal friend of mine, and he has approached me to see if I would be interested in using those dates for an exhibition of student work."

"The work would, of course, also be for sale

. . . at a price mutually agreeable to both artist and gallery. Those who don't wish to sell, may indicate this when they submit their work."

"Each student will be permitted to nominate up to three paintings for exhibition, with the final selection to be made by myself and the director. Naturally, as this is student work, no one will be expecting Michelangelos . . . and the art critics will be advised accordingly. But I am confident the standard of this class is such that we will be able to put together an interesting show. Any questions?"

One student put up her hand, and wanted to know what kind of prices they could expect for their work. Another asked about suitable framing. Manning said the gallery would look after the framing, and although prices were difficult to estimate at this stage, he would hazard a guess at a top of $500. Most of the works would probably fetch much lower, between $100 and $200.

"I'd give mine away, if someone wanted it," whispered David, as he looked ruefully at his half-finished still life of a bowl of fruit. "Did you ever see a banana like that one?" Helen smiled back at him.

The questions over, the class began painting. Manning moved from student to student, checking their work, and making suggestions. Sometimes he took the brush, and added a few deft strokes of his own.

When he came to Helen, he stopped to talk longer than with the others, praising the painting of Jim's garden.

"You've got it exactly now," he said. "Nice combination of light and shade . . . it has the feel of a Renoir. I like it."

Helen glowed under the praise, and she knew David had stopped painting and was listening to everything Lawrence Manning said.

"I want this one in the exhibition," he demanded, in his odd, peremptory tone. "Definitely. And go through anything else you have."

"Teacher's pet," muttered David, as Manning finally moved on. Helen gave him a playful flick with the handle of her brush.

"Jealousy will get you nowhere," she said. "Concentrate on your fruit salad."

* * *

As Helen thought, David was a smash hit when they went to dinner at the Robinsons.

The children warmed to him immediately, especially when he handed over a large box with a family game only just released on the market ("I did my homework," David whispered to Helen, as the children went into raptures over it.)

For Jim he had a bottle of very good red wine, and Anne he presented with flowers.

Helen could see that Jim liked him at once, by the warm handshake and the welcoming grin. David was definitely a man's man, thought Helen, as David and Jim got into a corner and started discussing business.

"All right, you two, break it up," said Helen. "No business talk until after dinner. That's an order."

David and Jim broke off their discussion, and rejoined the women."

"I was just telling Jim that if he'd like me to give a hand with anything . . . I'd be glad to do it," said David. "But he seems to have it well under control. It's a tricky business, going it on your own. Tried it once myself, and lost a packet."

Anne exchanged an anxious glance with Jim.

"I'm not going to take any risks," said Jim, aware of what Anne was thinking. "I can't, not with my family. Ross, my partner, has gone into it all thoroughly. The most we can lose is a lot of hard work, and I'm prepared for that. We reckon it will take at least a year, maybe two, before we start to see daylight."

"Who's your accountant?" asked David.

"He's not mine, he's done some work for Ross," said Jim. "Bob Lancaster, know him?"

"Good man," said David approvingly. "One of the best. You can't go wrong, if he's keeping an eye on things for you."

"Now what did I say about no business?" warned Helen. "You two can sit down and talk to your hearts' content later in the evening. Right now it's time to eat."

Helen led the way into the dining room, as Jim went out to the kitchen to see if he could give Anne a hand. Anne was a superb cook, even better than Helen, and had gone to special pains to make this dinner successful. A homemade soup, followed by rare roast beef with vegetables grown by Jim in their back garden, and a flaky-textured apple pie for dessert. Julie helped her mother by carrying the bowls of soup on a tray, and then clearing away the dirty dishes.

"She's quite the little housewife," commented David, as he watched Julie go back into the kitchen. "Dead ringer for her mother."

Helen agreed. Julie could be temperamental and difficult at times, not nearly as placid as either Scott or Paul. But she enjoyed doing things around the house, and was a great help to Anne through this pregnancy.

93

David complimented Anne on the meal, saying she must have ESP — roast beef was his favourite dish. His late wife used to cook it each Sunday. It was the only reference he made to Janet all evening, and he immediately went on to talk of other things. Helen found herself unaccountably curious about what kind of a woman Janet Barrington had been. She had pieced together some sort of picture, from the things David had told her, but there were still parts missing. Had they been very much in love . . . as much as she and Bill were? Was she content to stay home and be a housewife, or had she had career aspirations? Had they ever had arguments . . . and if so, about what? It was like putting together some giant jigsaw puzzle.

As soon as she started thinking these things, Helen became annoyed with herself. It was none of her business, after all. She didn't want to be like that mousy little creature in Rebecca, forever haunted by a memory. David's past life was his own affair.

The evening finally broke up, with handshakes and a warm invitation from Jim and Anne to come back again.

"He's nice, I like him," whispered Anne to Helen, as Jim helped David on with his coat.

Then it was into the car, and home to Helen's flat. Helen was happy the evening had turned out a success, and pleased her family approved of David. Still on a glow, she invited him in for a nightcap.

As they sat side by side on the sofa, drinks in hand, they discussed the coming art exhibition. David wasn't sure he had anything worth entering, but Helen assured him there were two or three pieces he should submit. She'd go through them with him, if he liked, and help him make a choice.

Helen's problem was more complex. She'd been painting on and off for years, and had a cupboard full of canvasses. She loved them all, and found it hard to choose which ones were her best.

"It's like trying to choose your favourite child," she explained. "The garden picture, that's a definite. But I'll go crazy trying to pick the rest."

As they were talking, David leaned over to put his empty glass on the coffee table. Their faces were very close together, and suddenly David took Helen in his arms and kissed her. Helen was too taken by surprise to do anything, but then found herself responding passionately.

She finally pulled away, and got to her feet.

"I'm sorry," she said, embarrassed. "I shouldn't have let that happen."

"I'm not sorry," said David. "You must know

95

how I feel about you.''

Helen made some excuse about being tired, and David reluctantly moved to the door.

"When will I see you again?'' he asked.

"I don't know,'' said Helen. She could feel her cheeks flush, and scolded herself. Stop it, she said. You're behaving like a lovesick teenager.

David kissed her again, this time more gently. Then with an "I'll call you!'' he was gone.

Helen leaned against the door, her eyes closed, the memory of David's kiss still with her.

She knew she should put a stop to the affair right now, before it went any further out of control. But she couldn't bring herself to do it. Somehow the evening at the Robinson house had set the seal of approval on the relationship, whatever that relationship might be. If Jim and Anne hadn't liked David, Helen felt she would have refused to go out with him again. But they had liked him. Very much. She knew they were expecting to see him again.

Helen decided not to worry any more, but just let it all happen. They were both adults, they knew what they were doing.

With that kiss, she had boarded an emotional roller coaster. But where would it all end??

Chapter 10

JUNE. And the baby is running late.

All the Robinson children had been born within a few days of the date the doctor predicted, but Anne was beginning to worry about this one. She was a week overdue, and starting to feel very uncomfortable. She tired easily, and wasn't getting much sleep. The last time she went to her doctor, he said he'd give her one more week, then book her in for an induction. But he assured her everything was fine.

"This one just needs cooking a little longer," he said, with a reassuring smile. "Don't worry, it will come when it wants to. They always do. Meantime, try and get as much rest as you can."

Anne reflected wryly on the doctor's advice as she went home. What she couldn't tell him was that Jim's business was taking up more of his time than he'd imagined, and most of the weight of running the household had fallen on Anne.

She didn't mind, because she knew how much the new business meant to him. But it was a strain at times, particularly when the children kept asking why daddy wasn't home. Jim left the house early each morning, sometimes before the rest of the family was up and about, and often didn't come home until after the young ones had gone to bed. Paul was usually up, doing his High School studies, but even he had gone three days without once sighting his father.

The worst time was at night, when Anne tried to lie still in bed and not disturb Jim with his sleep. He needed all he could get, and was already looking tired. But he told Anne new orders were coming in every day, and Ross was enthusiastic about their success.

"I'm sorry, darling," Jim would say night after night, as he collapsed into bed with exhaustion. "I know it's rough on you, but we've got to get on top. Just another few weeks, and I'll ease off . . . I promise."

Anne, desperately trying not to move around too much in the bed, and biting her lips as she felt the cramp pains go up her legs, would stand it for as long as she could. When it got too much, she would slip quietly out of the double bed, and go to the kitchen for a glass of warm milk. Sometimes she would sit there in the early hours, in her dressing gown, reading a book and waiting for the cramps to go.

Once or twice she felt a twinge that she thought could be labour pains. But they always went away.

Anne was not the only one suffering from Jim's new venture. When the children did see him, they found him short-tempered and irritable, inclined to snap at the smallest thing. Anne had played the role of the peacemaker, explaining to them that Jim was acting that way because he was tired. When she could, she kept them away from their father . . . bustling them out of the room when they became too boisterous and noisy. But the tension was starting to tell on everyone.

Anne thought once or twice of asking her mother for help. She knew she only had to speak up, and Helen would be over there in a flash. But the times when she'd spoken to Helen on the phone, she seemed to be so involved with her new friend David. They were going out almost every night together . . . to concerts, dinners, plays. And there was also the art exhibition. Helen had told Jim and Anne about it, and invited them to the opening. Anne just hoped she could last long enough to be there, before she had the baby. She knew Helen was excited about the prospect of her first public showing, and had spent a lot of time choosing the three she planned to exhibit. She hadn't shown them the paintings, but had told Anne that one would be a special surprise.

"Anyone home?"

It was Maria, putting her head around the kitchen door, as Anne sat at the table preparing dinner.

Anne hadn't seen Maria for a while, and welcomed the visit. She had been up to Queensland to visit her widowed mother and sister, leaving Max to fend for himself with the two boys. Scott had passed on word from Danny that Maria was due back today, and Anne had planned to call in to see her later.

Anne gave her friend and neighbour a warm hug, and put on the kettle for a cup of tea.

"I've missed you," she said. "How was the family?"

Maria shrugged.

"Fine," said said. "Mama has her days, some good . . . some not so good. You know how it is. But Anna takes good care of her."

Anne remembered meeting Maria's younger sister once, when she came down to Ramsay street for a visit. Slim, brown-haired, pleasant, with hardly a trace of accent. She had been born after her parents moved to Australia, and had gone to school in Queensland. She was quieter than Maria, less fiery and demonstrative. A nice girl.

Since their father died, she had stayed home to care for her mother. The European influence, thought Anne . . . they have a tradition of caring for their parents. She hoped it wouldn't mean Anne had to sacrifice any chance for marriage.

"So what's new with the Robinsons?" asked Maria, as they sat over their teas and cake.

Anne filled her in briefly on the latest happenings, including Helen's new suitor. Maria was delighted.

"Is it serious?" she asked.

"I'm not sure," said Anne. "But Jim and I are keeping our fingers crossed. We hardly see her these days, she's having a ball. And he's a very nice person."

As she was talking, Anne felt a sudden sharp twinge and winced in pain. Maria noticed, and was immediately concerned.

"Are you all right?" she asked, going over to Anne and putting her arm around her. "Shall I call Jim?"

Anne felt the pain throbbing through her body, and breathed deeply, trying to relax. Breathe in, breathe out . . . don't fight against it, go with it. Ahhhh, that was better . . .

But the strain still showed on her face, and Maria went to the phone. She had her hand on it, starting to dial, when Anne begged her not to.

"Please," she said. "Don't ring Jim, he's so busy these days. I don't want to drag him home for nothing. And it's gone now.It's just an early sign, I've had them before. If it comes on again, I'll ring the doctor."

Maria looked at her anxiously, her hand still on the phone.

"Promise?" she said.

Anne crossed her heart, starting to smile again. "Promise . . . Girl Guide's honour," she said. "Don't forget, I've already been through this three times before. You're talking to an expert in having babies."

Maria relaxed, and came back to the kitchen table."

"You gave me a fright there," she said. "You had me worried."

Anne pleaded with Maria not to let Jim know what had happened. He would only start to worry, and take time off from his business. And she couldn't allow him to do that. Maria finally promised to keep quiet, but warned she would speak up if it ever happened again.

"You're lucky, you know, Anne," she said,

her dark eyes clouding. "To have a husband who loves you like that."

Anne tried to treat the remark lightly, telling Maria that Max had been lost for the past week without her. Even Jim had commented old Max was mooning about the place, like a bear with a sore head. They'd asked him over a couple of times, but he'd refused.

"Bear with a sore head is right," said Maria. "He gave the boys a really bad time, especially Danny. Shane tells me he came home a couple of times, and found him in tears."

Anne knew what Maria was saying was right. Scott had told her more than once how unhappy Danny was, and had even suggested he stay at their place until Maria came back. But Jim had been against it, feeling it might cause more trouble.

"I'm sure it was just because Max was missing you," Anne said. "He doesn't show his feelings much . . . he probably took it out on the kids."

Maria looked unconvinced.

"It's not that," she said. "You know how hard Max always is with Danny."

"The trouble is, it's getting worse. I tell you, Anne, I'm worried sick. And I don't know what to do about it."

Chapter 11

"A FAMILY IN CRISIS"

HELEN and David walked along the street together, enjoying a brief patch of early winter sunshine. They had just dropped off their paintings at the gallery, ready for framing, and decided to leave the car and go for a stroll. The day was warm for the first week in June, and they both felt exhilarated by the coming exhibition.

David had finally settled on two small water colours he had done early in the course. They weren't impressive, but he felt they were at least respectable enough to go on public display. He and Lawrence Manning had jointly agreed that he had nothing else which would come up to standard.

Helen, on the other hand, had the garden painting, plus a seascape, and also a view of a mountain cottage where she had stayed on a painting holiday some years ago. Manning had suggested a fourth, but Helen had demurred . . .

saying that it would be unfair to the other students. She was more than happy with the three she'd chosen.

They came to a small outdoor cafe, with tables and striped umbrellas, and David suggested they have some afternoon tea. The cafe owner was European, probably Hungarian, Helen thought, as he took their order. David persuaded Helen to try some cherry strudel, while he settled for a layered torte.

"Well, now for a chance at fame and fortune," joked David, as they waited for their tea to arrive. "How do you fancy being Dame Helen?"

"I think I'll just settle for being a lazy amateur," said Helen. "But it's nice to think we're all going to have our work on show. The gallery owner seemed very pleasant. He said he'd known Lawrence since they worked together in Europe. Did you see that Manning picture on the back wall?"

David said he hadn't noticed, he'd been too busy looking around the place and wondering the best spot to hide his water colours. The washroom, maybe.

"Don't you dare!" said Helen, as the tea and cakes arrived with a Continental bow and a flourish. "Your paintings are just as good as all the others. In fact, I'm going to buy the small one . . . how d'you think it will look above my writing desk?"

"It's yours," said David. "Sold to the lady in the blue dress."

As they laughed and joked, enjoying each other's company, David suddenly took Helen's hand and became serious.

"I was going to talk to you tonight about this," he said. "But I can't wait that long."

Even before he said it, Helen knew what he was going to ask.

"I want to marry you," he said.

Helen's first, irrational reaction was . . . what a funny proposal. No mention of love, no declaration of undying passion, not even a "Will you . . .?" It was more a statement of fact. He wanted to marry her. How should she respond.

David took her silence as indecision, and quickly followed through with reasons why they should spend the rest of their lives together. They were both people on their own, who'd lost love ones. Both had had happy marriages, and knew the loneliness of living single lives.

They shared similar interests, he liked her family — and he was immodest enough to feel they liked him, too. He had a large house, she had a small flat. She could sell it, and move into his place. And of course, if she wanted to throw out all the old furniture and re-decorate it to her own taste, he'd be more than happy.

It was only the second time in Helen's life that a man had asked her to marry him.

She remembered back to the time when Bill had proposed. It had been just after she'd been expelled from school, and had returned in shame to her family.

It had been a painful time, with hurt and anger on both sides. She'd tried to explain to her parents that she was innocent, but they refused to listen. So she'd finally rushed out of the house in tears, and gone straight to the place were Bill was working.

Bill had been wonderful. He didn't ask for any explanations, he'd just taken her in his arms and kissed the tears away. Then he'd said just seven magic words: "I love you . . . let's get married now."

That was probably the happiest moment of her life . . . that, and when Anne was born. She didn't feel that same surge of emotion now. But then, she reminded herself sharply, she was also 33 years older.

David was pressing her for an answer. Helen abruptly switched her mind back to the present.

"We'd be so happy together, Helen," he urged. "Say yes."

Finally Helen promised to at least think about it. She told David it was too sudden, she couldn't think clearly right now. She needed at least the night to sleep on it.

David was still impatient for an answer, but finally agreed to wait. They walked back to the car, and he dropped her off at her flat, saying he'd ring her later. Just before she got out of his car, he kissed her.

"Please think about it," he said.

The phone was ringing as Helen entered her flat. For one wild moment she thought it was David, asking again for her answer. Then she realised he would still be in his car, driving back to his house.

"Hello," she said, picking up the receiver. "Helen Daniels speaking."

The voice at the other end was Anne's, and she sounded agitated. Not at all the calm, collected daughter that she knew.

"Are you all right, Anne? she asked. "Is it the baby?"

"It's not me, it's the children," said Anne. "Danny's run away from home."

Helen immediately remembered Maria's fears, her worry that Max's obsessive behaviour towards his younger son would eventually cause a crisis. So Maria had been right.

"Tell Maria I'm very sorry," she said. "If I can help, I'll come right over. Does Scott know where he's gone?"

Anne sounded in even more of a panic.

"That's why I'm ringing you," she said.

"Scott isn't home either. They've run away together."

Chapter 12

AT the Robinson and Ramsay houses, everything was in turmoil. Anne had rung Jim at his office, and he had dropped everything and rushed straight home. Max had been harder to find. He was on a plumbing job at a new house under construction, on the outskirts of the city, and it was nearly five o'clock before they could locate him.

When they did, his reaction was typically Max.

"Flamin' kids . . . they're more trouble than they're worth. I'll tan the hide off that Danny when I catch him."

Max's remark immediately sparked off an angry reaction from Maria, already tense from worry. She lashed out, blaming him for Danny having run away, and said it wouldn't have happened if he'd been half a father.

"What d'you mean?" bristled Max. "I feed and clothe him, don't I?"

"That's all you do," said Maria. "I've never once heard you say you love him. What about last night, the way you got stuck into him . . . all over nothing."

It turned out the 'nothing' had been Scott and Danny deciding to build a tree house, using Max's plumbing tools. They'd collected some old timber, and had nailed a few pieces together. Then Anne had called Scott in for dinner, leaving Danny on his own. When Max went to check his tool kit for work next day, his hammer was missing. He'd eventually found it lying in some wet grass and had torn strips off Danny, yelling at him and telling him he was useless. Shane had tried to stick up for Danny, but that had only made it worse. Danny had finally fled to his room, where Maria found him later in tears.

As the argument between Max and Maria grew to a shouting match, Jim stepped in to intervene.

"There's no point trying to work out whose fault it is," he said. "We're wasting time. What we've got to do is work out where they've gone, and find them."

It appeared neither Scott nor Danny had gone to school that day. They'd both left as usual, carrying their school bags and lunches. But a check with their teachers had established that neither had turned up.

111

Anne hadn't started to worry until Julie arrived home, saying she hadn't seen Scott all day. Then she'd found a note in his room, pencilled in his childish scrawl, saying: GONE WITH DANNY, DON'T WORRY. This had only made her worry more. She'd gone over to see Maria, and then rung Helen.

The four adults sat down together at the Robinson house, trying to work out a plan. Anne made cups of coffee, while Jim and Max talked through the possibilities.

Maria was all for calling the police, but Jim persuaded her to wait. He said he remembered running away himself when he was about Scott's age — he'd been living with an aunt, while his mother was on one of her overseas assignments. The aunt had made it clear she wasn't that pleased at being landed with a lively young boy to look after, and Jim had decided to leave home. He'd packed some food, and walked as far as the local park. Then he'd hung around there, playing, until it got dark. Some noise in the bushes had frightened him, and he'd gone back home again.

Jim's theory was that Scott and Danny would do the same. They were only wearing their school uniforms of shorts and shirts, not even a sweater, as the day had been warm. As soon as they got cold and hungry, they'd come home.

Anne wasn't so sure, but she agreed with Jim they shouldn't panic too quickly.

So Max and Jim decided to take Jim's car, drive around the local playgrounds and parks, and see if they could spot them. After all, how far could two seven-year-olds with no money go?

Helen arrived, just as Jim and Max were leaving. She put her arms around Maria and comforted her, telling her not to worry.Both Danny and Scott were sensible boys, they wouldn't do anything stupid. Helen's warmth and sympathy were the breaking point for Maria, already holding on tightly to her emotions. She clung to Helen, and burst into tears.

"Danny's so small," she sobbed. "Such a little boy. What if some stranger picks them up? You read every day about these things happening. They could be anywhere, dumped by the roadside. They could both be dead."

Privately Helen was starting to have some of the same worries herself. She knew how vulnerable young children could be, and there had been a couple of nasty incidents reported in the papers recently. But she didn't want to alarm Anne, particularly in her condition.

"I'm sure you're worrying over nothing," she said. "Jim and Max will find them, you'll see."

But Jim and Max came home an hour later on

their own. They'd searched every possible place, even gone back to Danny and Scott's school in the hope they might be hanging around the playground. But no sign of the two runaways. And now it was almost dark.

Shane had done the rounds of all Danny's school friends, hoping one of them could come up with some clue which would help. But he'd drawn a blank. Now he was eating dinner with Paul and Julie, at Anne's invitation.

She'd also asked Max and Maria, but Maria said she couldn't eat a thing, she was too worried. And Max said he'd pick up a meat pie later.He'd take the van and do one more search of the streets, taking in some areas he and Jim hadn't covered. Then if they still hadn't turned up, maybe Maria was right. Maybe they should call in the cops.

Maria went home with Shane. She wanted to be there in case Danny turned up, or someone rang with news. Helen walked over with her.

Julie and Paul went to their rooms to do homework. Jim put a comforting arm around Anne.

"How're you feeling, love?" he asked. This was the worst possible time for Anne to have a worry like this. She was overdue with the baby, suffering from lack of sleep, and looking tired and strained. Jim began to realise for the first time how much of a load Anne had been carrying on her own, with him as a part-time parent.

"I'm fine," said Anne. "But I'll feel better when I know where Scott is."

"This wouldn't have happened if I'd been home a bit more," said Jim, bringing his guilt feeling out into the open. "Scott must've known how Danny was feeling. We've always been good mates, he would have warned me. Then I could have done something."

"You said yourself, there's no point in blaming anyone," said Anne. "You can't help it if you've got to work long hours. The children understand, they accept it."

"I still think part of this is my responsibility," insisted Jim. "If I'd been around a bit more to keep an eye on things . . . it's been hard for you, hasn't it?"

"No harder than it's been for you," said Anne, kissing him. "We're in this together, remember? We both agreed to make sacrifices, so you could get the business established. Stop blaming yourself."

But Jim couldn't get rid of the thought that if he'd been home more often, he would have seen all this coming. He resolved then and there that once Danny and Scott were found, he would try to spend more time with his family.

*   *   *

Ten o'clock. And still no word from Danny or Scott.

By this time the police had been notified. But they told Max and Jim they couldn't do much, beyond tell their patrol cars to keep a lookout for the runaways. If the boys hadn't turned up by the morning, then they'd organise a wider search.

Julie had gone to bed, but Paul insisted on staying up. Helen was also there. The four sat in the living room, jumping every time there was a noise outside or the phone rang.

"If Scott would only ring and at least let us know he's safe," Jim said over and over again. He was beginning to share some of Maria's fears about the boys being abducted. If they'd been in an accident, they'd have heard from a hospital by now. Scott was such a sensible kid, and knew his mother's condition. It wasn't like him to put them through so much worry.

"Well, look on the bright side," said Helen, trying to keep up morale. "They're only young, they can't get too far on foot. If they were teenagers, you'd have something to worry about. By this time they'd be in a car and a few hundred miles away. Anyone for a cuppa?"

She was walking to the kitchen, as Jim and Anne talked quietly between themselves and Paul sat frowning.

116

Suddenly Paul jumped to his feet, excited.

"I've got it!" he said. "I know where they are."

Jim stopped talking and turned to look at him.

"The car," said Paul. "They're in the car."

"What're you talking about?" asked Jim.

Paul explained that one day when he'd been out with Scott and Danny, they'd come across a vacant allotment on which someone had dumped a car. The car was old and rusting, but Danny and Scott had taken turns at the wheel, pretending they were racing drivers.

Danny had commented that it would make a great hideaway, but at the time Paul hadn't taken much notice of it. Now he was certain that's where they'd be.

Jim decided not to tell Max and Maria, in case it proved to be a false trail. Instead, he would go in the car with Paul and check it out.

They took torches, and a couple of blankets. Anne wanted to come with them, but Jim insisted she stay home with Helen. She'd had enough excitement for one day . . . besides, it might just finish up in disappointment.

Paul directed Jim to the vacant allotment, not more than five minutes drive from the Robinson house. Jim parked the car and got out. He decided not to turn on his torch yet, in case he alarmed the boys and they panicked and ran.

The two walked to the rusty old car and peered inside. At first they thought it was empty. Then they made out the two boys, huddled close together for warmth, on the back seat.

As soon as Jim flashed the torch, Scott woke up. He climbed out of the car and into Jim's arms.

"I knew you'd find me," he said. Jim held him tight.

Danny followed more reluctantly, looking around for Max.

"It's all right, your parents are home," said Jim. "You're not going to get into trouble."

When they arrived at the Ramsay house, Jim had a quiet word with Max as Maria rushed and took Danny in her arms, smothering him with kisses.

"Don't be too hard on the kid," Jim said. "He's been through enough."

So Max surprised Maria by being exceptionally restrained, merely commenting again that kids were more trouble than they were worth, and he hoped Danny was sorry for all the worry he'd caused the Robinsons. Then saying he had an early job to get to in the morning, he went to bed.

Maria gave Danny a hot bath, and put him in

warm pyjamas. Then she fed him, and listened while he told her all his adventures. He and Scott had wandered around for a while, looking in shop windows. They had both raided their piggy banks, and had eighty cents between them. When they got hungry, they'd bought some chips from a fish and chips shop. But that had been around midday. They hadn't had anything else to eat until now.

"You frightened the life out of me," said Maria, holding him close to her. "Promise me you'll never do anything silly like that again."

At the Robinson house, it was all hugs and kisses for the returning prodigal son. Anne had rushed to the door as soon as she heard Scott's voice, and when the door opened, he ran into her arms.

There were no recriminations, no lectures. Jim knew the only reason Scott had run away was to keep his best friend company. He knew how strong the bonds of mateship could be, particularly at that age.

Julie was woken up and told the good news. Paul had a meal with Scott, and then the two went off to the bedroom they shared together.

Later, Jim and Anne went in to check the sleeping Scott, and tuck the bedclothes around him. The two had a bunk bed, with Paul on the upper bunk and Scott down below. Paul stirred, as Jim and Anne were standing there, and put his head over the top to see what was happening.

"Go back to sleep, it's only us," said Jim.

Then as he got to the door, he added: "And thanks, mate, for helping us find them."

Anne also went to bed, saying she'd sleep well tonight. The strain of the last few hours had left her exhausted. Jim offered to drive Helen home, but she said she wanted to talk to Maria first.

Maria was in the kitchen, sitting quietly on her own, when Helen knocked at the back door.

"Just thought I'd pop in to see if everything is all right," she said.

Maria's sombre look brightened as soon as she saw Helen, and she jumped up to make some coffee. But Helen waved her back, saying she'd had enough cups of black coffee during the runaway crisis to last her for a year.

"Why did Danny run away?" she asked.

Maria shrugged. "Same old story," she said. "You know Max, he's always picking on poor Danny. I guess Danny couldn't take it any more."

Helen hesitated, then decided to take the plunge.

"Don't you think it's time Max knew the truth?" she asked.

120

Maria's face tightened. "Never!" she said. "And I don't want you to say anything, either."

Helen put her hand on Maria's. "You know I'd never betray a trust," she said. "Our friendship means too much for that. If you don't want Max to know, then that's fine with me. I just thought it might make things easier for Danny."

"The trouble is, it might make it worse," said Maria. She sighed. "Sometimes I wonder why Max and I ever got married. It seemed a good idea at the time . . . he was very good to my family. But now, I'm not so sure."

"You married for all the right reasons," Helen assured her.

Maria still looked worried.

"I honestly don't know, Helen," she said.

"But I tell you one thing. A marriage for the wrong reasons is in big trouble. A real marriage needs to be based on love."

Chapter 13

NEXT day Helen turned down David Barrington's proposal.

Instead of phoning, he'd come around early in the morning, anxious to know if she'd thought again about the two of them getting married. Helen toyed with the idea of breaking it gently and diplomatically, then decided there was no point.

"I'm sorry, David," she said. "The answer is no."

David didn't give up without a battle. At first he wanted to know her reasons, saying he was entitled to that much. Helen's answer was simple. She couldn't marry him, because she'd loved Bill too much.

The answer astounded David. He protested, saying he'd also loved Janet. Marriage wouldn't mean betraying memories of the past. Besides, he added, they should both be realistic at their age. Neither was exactly a spring chicken any-

122

more, and marriage would give them companionship in the later years of their life. It could be lonely growing old on one's own.

As he talked, Helen thought he sounded exactly like the accountant he was . . . weighing up the debits and credits on each side, and coming out with a balance on the bottom line. She didn't know whether to laugh or cry.

Instead, she told him gently that she felt marriage should be more than just an insurance for old age. There should be love as well.

David looked at her in surprise. Surely she didn't expect them to behave like a couple of romantic teenagers, mooning about all the time? And he was sorry if he'd put it badly. Of course there would be more to it than companionship. Helen was a very attractive woman. He'd grown more than fond of her.

"And I'm fond of you, too," said Helen. "Very much. If it's any consolation, you're the only man I've had any serious thoughts about since Bill died. But it's not the same as being in love . . . I can't accept a compromise."

David started to get angry.

"I didn't look on myself as a compromise," he said. "You led me to believe you felt the same way I did."

Helen sighed. This was proving more difficult than she thought.

"I never meant to hurt you, David," she said. "I'm sorry."

He didn't try and talk her into it any more. Instead, he picked up his hat and walked out of the flat and her life.

*　　*　　*

The day of the art exhibition arrived. Jim and Anne came along, and admired all three of Helen's paintings. They were in a prominent position on the wall of the modern, well-lit gallery, and listed in the catalogue simply as Spring Flowers, Ocean View, Mountain Cottage, by H. Daniels.

Jim immediately wanted to buy the painting of Anne in the garden, but Helen said it wasn't for sale. She'd gladly give it to him when the exhibition was over.

Anne smiled when she saw it.

"So this was the surprise," she said. "Was I ever as thin as that?"

Helen looked around for David, but he wasn't there. His two water colours were on another wall, and one had a red sticker on it. It was the one she'd told him she might buy to hang above her writing desk. Helen wondered if the 'buyer' might have been David himself, to spare her embarrassment.

They wandered around for a while, admiring the pictures, with Helen stopping every now and then to chat to some of her painting colleagues. Lawrence Manning was there, and came across with a smile on his face as soon as he saw Helen. She introduced him to Jim and Anne.

"This is a very talented lady," he told them. "My star pupil. I expect great things of her."

Helen protested, saying she still had a lot to learn. But she was pleased at the praise, especially coming from such a master. Later she showed Jim and Anne the Manning painting hanging at the rear of the gallery. It was the private possession of the gallery owner, and was marked Not For Sale. Jim stood back, and admired the strong, bold colours.

"Not exactly my cup of tea," he said. "But I can see why he's famous."

Later, back at the Robinson house, Helen told them about David's proposal, saying she'd decided against it, but adding quickly that they were still good friends. Jim said he was glad about that, David seemed a nice bloke. Intelligent, and with his head screwed on the right way. Anne's reaction was one of disappointment.

"Just when I'd worked out what dress I was going to wear to the wedding," she said. "Are you sorry?"

"Of course not," said Helen. "What on earth would I do with a husband at my age? I've got enough on my plate right now, without any more complications."

"Like what?" demanded Anne.

"My Community Centre work, one day a month at the church, cooking, painting, visiting my grandchildren. Don't forget I'm coming to stay here any day now. I wouldn't have time to fit in a husband."

"You do too much for us," said Anne. "I worry about it sometimes. You should start thinking of yourself more . . . we love seeing you, but you deserve a life of your own."

"Stuff and nonsense," said Helen. "And if you've got any thoughts that I turned down David because of helping you, forget it. I did it because I felt we weren't right for each other. And I love coming here, you know that."

"And we love having you," said Anne, hugging her mother.

Later, over dinner, they talked about Jim's new venture. Jim said it was going well, although slowly, and he felt he could afford to ease off a little now. After that escapade with Scott and Danny, he had made a point of trying to get home each night before the children went to sleep, even if it was just to sit on their beds

126

and ask them what they'd been doing that day.

Anne, for once, was feeling good. The cramps had eased, and she now felt the worst was over. Just a few more days . . . Looking at her, Jim thought he'd never seen her more beautiful. She had that glow about her that comes with motherhood.

"Just think," said Anne, "This time next week, there could be six Robinsons."

They talked again about names, and whether the baby would be a boy or a girl. Julie badly wanted a little sister.

"It's horrible being the only one," she said. "If it's a girl, I can give her my dolls."

Jim took Helen home to her flat. When he got back, Anne was just getting ready for bed.

"How do you fancy a cruise of the Greek islands, Mrs Robinson?" he said, putting his arms around her.

Anne thought he was joking.

"Sure, and a trip to the moon as well," she said.

But Jim wasn't joking. He told Anne that he and Ross had gone through their future projections, and if business continued to improve the way it was doing, they could stop scrimping and saving in a couple of years.

His thought was that he and Anne would take off on their first overseas holiday — maybe not the Greek isles, perhaps somewhere closer like Bali or Fiji. Helen obviously enjoyed being with the children, and he was sure she wouldn't mind living in for a week or two.

"I want this to be a second honeymoon," he said. "After all these years, you deserve it. Just the two of us, on our own."

As they lay in each other's arms in the darkness, Jim reflected on his good fortune. A job that he loved, a wife in a million, three — almost four — beautiful children, a home in a street with friendly neighbours.

Yes, thought Jim, life for the Robinson family couldn't be more perfect.

Chapter 14

HELEN was at her art class, and feeling unexpectedly low in spirits. The place next to her was empty . . . David hadn't turned up. And she hadn't heard from him since the day he walked out of her flat.

Although she was certain she'd made the right decision, Helen couldn't help a sense of regret. She enjoyed David's company, and missed it. He had been a charming and interesting dinner companion, talking about the countries he'd visited and the places he'd seen.

Then there were the concerts. Although Helen sometimes managed to rope in a friend to go with her, single people of her age group were few and far between. They were nearly all married, busy with their own families and interests. She'd gone once or twice on her own, when it had been a musician she'd especially wanted to hear. But it wasn't the same as having someone to talk to, and exchange opinions.

Yes, she had to be honest with herself. She definitely missed him.

As she was musing, applying brush strokes to her latest work, Lawrence Manning came over.

"Mr Barrington not here today, I see," he said, looking at the vacant space. "Strange, and he seemed so enthusiastic."

Helen said that perhaps he wasn't well. There was a lot of flu going around at the moment.

"Anyway, that's not why I came to talk to you," said Manning. "Could you stay behind after class? There's something I want to discuss."

*   *   *

At the Robinson house, Anne was doing the laundry. She was sitting at the kitchen table, sorting the dirty clothes, and frowning over a tear in Scott's jeans, when Maria walked in.

"Hi," said Maria. "I'm on my way to the hairdresser, then I'm going to the supermarket. Anything you want?"

Anne thanked her for the offer, but said Jim had stocked up on groceries just the day before. He'd bought extra, in case she went into labour soon. Anne asked how things were going between Max and Danny. Maria pulled a face.

"Don't ask," she said. "You know Max. He

means well, but he can't help losing his temper. I'll give him one thing, though. Since the night Danny ran away, he's been really trying. Danny's been good, too. Just keep your fingers crossed it's going to last."

Anne held up the jeans, with the big three-cornered rip in one leg.

"Boys!" she said. "What d'you do with something like this? I'm a bit with Julie, I hope this one's going to be a girl."

Maria smiled and left, and Anne walked to the laundry and started loading the machine.

*   *   *

The painting class had finished, and the students were packing up their easels and filing out of the room.

Helen waited behind, and Lawrence Manning came over to her. "Let's go to my office," he said.

Helen had been in his office only once before, when she'd enrolled for his course. It looked like the office of an artist, untidy and cluttered, with books and papers scattered everywhere, and a layer of dust on the desk. A couple of canvasses were propped against one wall. A piece of art paper pinned to a noticeboard had the schedule of classes ... Beginner, Semi-Advanced, Advanced, Mixed. Helen's class was a mixed one. She was more comfortable working with people of varying ability; it felt less competitive.

"Sit down," Manning invited, moving a couple of books from a chair. "I suppose you're wondering why I want to talk to you."

"Is it about the exhibition?" asked Helen. "If it's someone who wants to buy a painting, I'm sorry, but I don't want to sell anything. Maybe I'm selfish, but I'd like to keep them for myself."

"It's about the exhibition, yes," said Manning. "But not about selling a painting."

He went on to tell her that she'd been selected for an art scholarship, on the basis of her work at the exhibition — and also his personal recommendation. The scholarship was for one year in Paris, all expenses paid, including air fare. She would study and work in one of France's most famous art establishments, spending her time between a studio on the Left Bank and touring the great art galleries.

"How soon would you be prepared to leave?" asked Manning. "They're anxious for you to go as soon as possible. Just give me a date, and I'll arrange the air booking."

Helen said she had a family commitment to

mind her grandchildren, while her daughter went into hospital. But she would be free after that.

"Fine, I'll be in touch," said Manning, as he shook her hand and ushered her to the door. "And congratulations, Mrs Daniels. I went to Paris myself on a scholarship, when I was in my twenties. It was the best thing that ever happened to me as an artist. I know you'll love it."

Helen was still in shock as she walked back to her apartment building. Paris . . . and for a whole year! It was something she'd always dreamed about, but never thought possible. And now it had all happened.

For a moment she thought of ringing David to tell him. It was only a momentary impulse, and she soon rejected it. He might misinterpret the call, and think she was making overtures to get back to their old relationship. No, she'd ring Anne instead.

*　　*　　*

In the laundry, Anne had done one load of washing and was preparing for the second. She emptied the machine and put the wet clothes into a laundry basket. Then she reached up to a shelf for some more washing powder.

As she reached, she felt a sudden, sharp pain in her belly. Then the room started to swim around her. Anne tried to steady herself, holding on to the side of the washing machine. She could hear the phone ringing in the kitchen, but she didn't have the strength to get to it. Anne made one more effort to stay on her feet, then collapsed unconscious on the floor.

Chapter 15

HELEN rang Anne a couple of times, then gave it up as a bad job. She must be out shopping, she thought. Or in the garden, where she couldn't hear the phone.

The thought of shopping reminded Helen that she needed some groceries. As she walked through the lanes of the supermarket, filling her basket, she began to fantasise. She was shopping at one of the Paris markets, bargaining in her schoolgirl French for cheese and croissants and those long crusty loaves.

Helen found it hard to believe that in another month or sooner, she'd be walking the streets of the most exciting city in the world. Exciting for an artist, that is. Strolling through the Louvre, studying the Great Masters. Sitting at the sidewalk cafes, sipping coffee. Riding the Metro. Watching the young lovers stroll arm in arm along the Champs Elysee.

She was still daydreaming when she reached

the checkout counter, and came down to earth with a start when she heard the girl say in a broad Australian accent: "That'll be fifteen dollars twenty." Helen paid, packed her groceries into two plastic carry bags, and went home.

The phone was ringing as she struggled with the parcels and her keys to let herself into the flat. It stopped just as she got to it, then as she turned to go to the kitchen, it started again.

It was Jim, to tell her that Anne had been rushed to hospital. Could she come over immediately, and mind the children when they came home from school?

Helen at first thought Jim meant Anne had gone into labour, and made some joking remark about the fourth one being the fastest. But a distraught Jim said Anne had been rushed to the hospital for a caesarian, after a neighbour found her collapsed on the floor. And it wasn't straightforward . . . there were complications.

At the hospital, Jim waited anxiously in a waiting room near the operating theatre. A nurse offered him a cup of tea, but he shook his head. He didn't feel like having anything until he was sure Anne was okay.

There was another father in the waiting room, a young man in his early twenties. "First one?" he asked, as Jim got up from his seat once more to pace around.

136

"Fourth," said Jim shortly, not anxious to get into conversation with a stranger.

"First time for me," said the young man. "They say it gets easier as you go on. My wife's having twins."

Anne's doctor appeared at the door, and beckoned Jim into the corridor. "Congratulations, Mr Robinson," he said. "You're the father of a healthy baby girl."

Jim's first thought was for Anne. The doctor reassured him that his wife was doing fine. She was still in the recovery room coming out of the anaesthetic. But in another twenty minutes or so, Jim could talk to her.

The new baby was in a bassinet alongside Anne's bed when he visited her in the hospital room. It had been larger than the other three, nearly eight pounds, a pink crinkled little old woman wrapped in a white blanket. Anne was pale, but smiling.

"Now we've evened up the family," she said. "Two boys, two girls."

Jim sat alongside Anne and held her hand for another hour or two, the baby sleeping peacefully beside them. They talked about names again, and decided on Lucy. It had been Anne's first choice, after a favourite character in a childhood storybook.

"She looks like a Lucy," said Anne, in an illogical way that mothers have.

Jim told Anne that Helen was minding the children. He would go back with her to the flat, and pick up her clothes.

Then there was the birth notice to be put in the paper, and friends to be told. Tomorrow the children would visit the hospital and meet their new baby sister. And in another ten days, Anne would be coming home.

"Did I tell you how much I love you?" said Jim, kissing Anne on the forehead. "I was worried sick when I heard what had happened."

"Who'd have thought a little thing like that could give me such a bad time," wondered Anne, looking at the tiny scrap of humanity alongside her. She reached out a hand, and touched the dark hair on Lucy's head. The baby stirred, opened her eyes for a moment, then went back to sleep again . . . still in that half life between womb and world.

Anne began to get sleepy herself, the effects of the anaesthetic still with her. When she closed her eyes, Jim kissed her once more and tip-toed out of the room.

Chapter 16

NEXT morning, the Robinson children were
jumping out of their skins with excitement. This was the day they'd been looking forward to, the day when they would visit their
mother and baby sister.

Helen had trouble getting them off to school,
with Julie demanding they should get the day
off. Helen reminded her she'd already arranged
with their teachers for them to have an early
mark, as visiting hours were between two and
three in the afternoon.

Jim had loaned her his car, and Helen
planned to pick up the children from the two
schools, then drive to the modern brick maternity annexe recently added to the Erinsborough
Hospital.

But as she was getting ready after lunch to go
and collect them, she had a phone call from
David Barrington.

It felt strange to hear his voice again, after

five days of silence. He said he'd been ringing her at the flat all morning, and when he didn't get an answer he remembered her saying she'd be moving to the Robinson house while Anne was in hospital.

"So what was it, a boy or girl?" he asked.

Helen filled him in on the details, and told him both Anne and the baby were doing well. David asked her to pass on his good wishes.

There was a painful pause, with Helen holding the receiver and wondering what to say. Then David told her he'd run into Lawrence Manning, who had told him the good news about Helen's art scholarship.

"I couldn't be more delighted," said David warmly. "You deserve it . . . congratulations. Jim and Anne must be very proud."

Helen admitted she hadn't got around to telling them. Everything had happened so fast, what with Anne being rushed to hospital, and then packing up and moving in, it had gone right out of her mind.

She said she'd probably say something when everything settled down and life was more back to normal. Meantime, how were things with David?

David hesitated, then said he had some news of his own. Helen wouldn't be the only one travelling overseas. He planned to visit a cousin living in Canada, and would be away indefinitely. He was putting his house on the market, as there wasn't much point in leaving it empty. And he didn't fancy tenants. When he ran into Manning, he had told him he wouldn't be coming back to the art classes.

"I was never much of a student, anyway," he said. "I won't be missed."

Helen was about to say she'd miss him, but decided it might be taken the wrong way. She felt annoyed with herself for having to choose her words so carefully. She was normally an honest and straightforward person, and it went against her nature to act like this. But somehow the old relaxed friendship between her and David had been lost.

They exchanged a few more pieces of polite conversation, and then there was another awkward silence. It was broken by David, who suddenly said: "This is silly . . . anyone would think we were a couple of strangers. You must know why I'm going away."

"I hope it isn't because of me," said Helen, knowing it was.

David then told her he would be flying out in two weeks. His plane left at 8.00 am. He asked her to think carefully again about his marriage proposal, and gave her a phone number where she could contact him.

141

"I do think the world of you, Helen," he said. "Maybe it's not what you call love, but it's near enough for me. I still think we could have a wonderful life together."

"Now don't say anything right now," he added quickly, as Helen began to speak. "I don't want to pressure you, because I know you've got a lot on your plate right now. But if you change your mind and decide to say 'yes', I'll cancel the trip like a shot. Just promise me you'll at least think carefully about it."

So Helen promised, and put the piece of paper with David's phone number in her pocket. Then she deliberately put him out of her mind. Her own life could wait. Right now, the most important person in the world was her beautiful new granddaughter Lucy.

*   *   *

Anne was sitting up in bed when they arrived, looking relaxed and happy. She had lost the tiredness and tension, and her cheeks were back to their normal healthy pink. She was wearing a pretty blue flowered nightgown with matching bed jacket, and on the table alongside her was a vase of white roses . . . a gift from Jim.

Scott immediately bounded over, jumped on the bed, and gave his mother a hug and kiss. Julie and Paul were less demonstrative, awed by the hospital surroundings. Julie went straight to the bassinet and looked at the new baby.

"Does it cry much?" she asked her mother.

"She," corrected Anne automatically. "No, she's a very good baby. Just like you all were."

"She's so tiny," marvelled Julie, touching the tiny curled fingers. "She could wear my dolls' clothes."

Helen had also brought flowers for Anne, and went off to look for a vase for them. Before she left, she took Lucy from Julie and tucked her back in the bassinet.

Anne hugged the children to her . . . she'd only been away one day, but already she was missing them. "So what's been happening?" she asked.

They all began talking at once, telling her the latest news from school and Ramsay Street.

"I told about the baby in Show and Tell," said Scott. "The whole class clapped. Show and Tell was a weekly session, in which the children passed on news and anecdotes about their families and friends.

Paul said he was going with Shane to Max's training session at the pool tomorrow. Max had told him he could help with the timing. And Julie told Anne she'd started to knit a jacket for the baby. "I found this really nice pattern in a magazine," she said. "It's all lacey . . . Gran's helping me with it."

"She doesn't need much help . . . she's doing a very nice job of it," commented Helen, as she walked back into the room and caught the last part of the conversation. She put the vase of flowers near Jim's roses.

"How's Jim?" asked Anne.

"Working his head off as usual," said Helen. "But he said to tell you he'll be around this evening. And the Warners will be visiting in a couple of days."

Helen remembered the call from David, and passed on his message of good wishes.

"Are you sure that's all he rang you for?" said Anne, eyeing her mother shrewdly. "Don't tell me you two are getting back together again?"

Helen denied it, saying it was all over. They were just good friends. But she could feel her cheeks getting pink as she said it. Stop it, she scolded herself. This is ridiculous. But that telephone call from David had definitely put her off balance.

Back home again, the children changed out of their school uniforms and went off to play.

Helen began preparing an early dinner, so Jim could eat as soon as he got home from work, and then dash off to the hospital.

As she was peeling vegetables, Maria came over to hear the latest news of the baby. Helen filled her in, and they sat down to have a cup of coffee together. As they talked, it started to rain heavily. Then the rain turned to hail. Helen got up to call the children inside, but Maria told her not to worry. They were over at the Ramsay house with Shane and Danny, watching television.

"This reminds me of the night Danny was born," said Maria, looking at the window as the hail turned to wet again. "It was raining then, d'you remember? You should — you were minding Shane for me."

Helen's mind went back to that night seven years ago. She had been baby-sitting for Jim and Anne, shortly before Scott had been born. She remembered it clearly, because Anne at first hadn't wanted to go out. But she and Jim had talked her into it, saying it would be the last chance the two would have for a quiet evening on their own. Finally Jim had booked the restaurant, a new and very elegant one that had only just been opened. Anne had looked beautiful that night, Helen remembered, although she was seven months pregnant. And Jim had bought her a corsage of flowers.

When they'd come home later in the pouring rain, Jim sheltering Anne's head with his coat as they dashed from the driveway to the house, they'd found Shane curled up asleep on the couch . . . and Helen looking after him.

Helen explained that Maria had gone into labour, and Max had brought Shane over . . . asking if she could look after him while he drove Maria to hospital. Max said he wouldn't be long, just time enough to settle in Maria.

Max didn't like hospitals, and made no bones about it. They made him nervous. And he wasn't the type to hang around and hold Maria's hand, he left that kind of thing to the doctors and nurses. After all, they were being paid for it.

Danny was born in the early hours of the morning, just as the rain eased off. At breakfast, Max came over to tell them. Jim commented at the time that he didn't seem too excited by Danny's birth, but Anne put it down to Max's unemotional nature.

"Deep down, I bet he's thrilled," she said. "And don't forget, it's the second one. Parents always tend to go overboard about the first."

"Not this one," said Jim. "So far as I'm concerned, it gets better every time."

Maria's face clouded, as they talked about it.

146

"Sometimes I envy Anne," she said. "She and Jim always seem so happy. If only Max would accept Danny, and show that he loves him . . ."

"I'm sure he does," Helen assured her. "But I still think you're doing the wrong thing by hiding the truth from him. Why don't you just tell him?"

*   *   *

The truth . . .

September, 1967. The month of spring. And the day of Max and Maria's wedding anniversary. Max, for some reason, had been in a foul mood. He'd had work problems, and had taken out his anger on Maria. And he'd also been drinking heavily at the pub during the afternoon.

Anne and Jim had been away on holiday with the children. Helen had offered to mind Shane at her flat, so that Max and Maria could go out and celebrate with dinner. Maria dropped him off late in the afternoon, and showed Helen the new dress she planned to wear that night.

But when Max came home, he didn't like it. He told Maria it was too revealing, too provocative, and accused her of deliberately trying to

147

attract other men. Normally Maria could cope with Max's jealousy, and laugh it off. But this time she couldn't break through his black mood. When she refused to change the dress, he'd gone back to the pub.

Normally after a drinking bout, Max always came home to sober up. But this time he stayed away all night.

Next morning, Maria went to the hotel to look for him. The barman told her that Max was upstairs in one of the bedrooms, sleeping it off.

But when she moved towards the staircase, the barman called her back. Embarrassed, he told her that Max was not alone . . . there was a woman with him.

Hurt and outraged, Maria fled home again. She'd asked Helen to look after Shane for a few days, while she went away to think her marriage through. Helen had agreed, although with some misgivings.

At a small country guest house Maria nursed her pain and anger. There, she met a man . . . Tim Duncan. They'd been immediately attracted to each other, and had a brief, passionate affair. He was a more sensitive lover than Max, and brought out passions and feelings Maria never knew she had. But the main reason for going to bed with him was to hit back at Max.

They parted, agreeing never to meet again. Maria had gone back to Max, in an effort to keep together her marriage . . . for Shane's sake. Then she'd found she was pregnant.

Nine months later, Danny was born. Maria knew for certain that Max was not the father — it was Tim Duncan. The problem was . . . did Max guess it also?

It was a question that was to haunt Maria's marriage from then on.

*   *   *

Later, after Maria had gone home, Helen thought about their talk. Maria was right in envying Jim and Anne their happiness. From the first time Anne had brought Jim home to meet her parents, Helen had known this would be the man for her.

Anne wasn't the kind of girl who liked to flirt, or play around. She had been out with boys a few times, but nothing serious. Until she met Jim. Helen, with the instinct that comes from being a mother, could sense immediately Jim was important to her. She could tell from Anne's face when she talked about him, the way she'd look at Jim when he came to their home for dinner.

So it hadn't come as a surprise when Anne woke them up one night and said that Jim had asked her to marry him.

Bill had been dead against it at first, saying they were both too young to know their own minds. Besides, Jim was still a student. Why couldn't they wait until he graduated and had a job?

Helen also had her misgivings. But she'd been won over by Jim's commonsense and mature outlook, and their obvious love for each other. When Anne pleaded with her to give permission, Helen had finally given in . . . and persuaded Bill to do the same. She had argued that their daughter's happiness should be their first consideration.

After all, as Helen pointed out, she had been a child bride herself — only sixteen. And their love had lasted all that time — a perfect marriage.

Perfect . . .

Helen couldn't help thinking about David again. She had been blessed with a wonderful husband, and years of happiness. Could it happen twice in a lifetime?

Chapter 17

THE next four days passed calmly and uneventfully in the Robinson household. Each morning, Helen got the children off to school, and then did the rounds of the bedrooms and bathroom collecting dirty laundry. She would do a load of washing, hang out soggy towels on the line, and then sit down and make a checklist of what food she needed to buy for the day.

Around ten, she would have a break for coffee. Sometimes she went over to visit Maria, other times Maria came to her. It was nice to get back to their old, companionable friendship.

In the afternoons, Helen went to the hospital to visit Anne and Lucy. She would be home in time to greet the three children, and hear all their news from school. Dinner was always early, so Jim could have as much time as possible with his wife and new baby daughter. In the evenings, Helen helped with the homework and prepared school lunches for the next day.

It was a busy routine, that sometimes left her tired at the end of the evening. She'd almost forgotten how demanding three young and lively youngsters could be.

In between, she thought of David.

Although she had been the one to break off the relationship, she had to admit she was missing him. It had been very pleasant these past few weeks, dining at restaurants, going to plays and concerts. He was a charming companion, intelligent, well-read. And he made her feel less of a mother and grandmother, and more like a woman again. Helen had almost forgotten how important a man in one's life could be.

If she never saw him again, she would be very sorry. She thought of his plane flying out to Canada, and the thought brought a lump to her throat.

Maybe David was right after all. They had both had perfect love, and nothing could destroy those memories. But couldn't a marriage based on friendship and common interests work just as well?

Jim came home from the hospital, after visiting Anne, and reported that mother and baby were doing fine. But Anne was getting impatient with being in hospital, and looking forward to coming home.

She had four more days to go, before being

discharged. Would Helen mind packing a small suitcase with baby clothes, and also one of Anne's pre-maternity dresses? Jim gave Helen a list of what was needed.

Jim took out his briefcase, and retreated to the living room to work on some blueprints. The first orders were starting to come in for the engineering workshop. Helen mended a pair of Paul's socks, and signed a permission note for Julie to go on a school outing.

At ten, she decided to go to bed. Jim was still working on his papers, and she took him a cup of coffee.

"It's going well, Helen," he said. "If we can just survive the first year, I think we'll be fine. But it's going to mean a lot of sacrifices."

"I'm sure it will work out in the long run," said Helen. "The main thing is that you're doing what you want to do. That's important."

As Helen turned to go to her bedroom, Jim called her back.

"We appreciate what you're doing for us," he said. "Thanks, Helen."

Helen smiled, said it was nothing, and went to her room.

She was undressing for bed, when she put a hand in her pocket and felt the piece of paper with David's phone number on it. Helen took it out and looked at it again. And she remembered something Bill had said to her, those last days when he knew he was dying.

"Don't grieve for me too long, sweetheart," he'd said. "Growing old on your own can be very lonely. If you meet someone else and have a chance to be happy, take it. Just make sure he's the right one for you."

Then and there, Helen decided David Barrington was the right one. She decided to ring him first thing in the morning and accept his proposal of marriage. And yes, in a kind of a way, it was almost love. They could be very happy together.

Having decided, Helen felt a great weight lifted from her mind. From now on, she'd have someone to share her problems. Someone to be close to in the darkness of the night, talking through the things that happened to both of them. She could still take up the art scholarship and go to Paris . . . they could do the trip together. David had said many times how much he'd like to go back to France again.

Relaxed, thinking of the new future opening up for her, Helen closed her eyes and fell asleep almost immediately.

Jim worked until midnight, then made himself a warm drink and turned in. He read for a while, then drifted off to sleep, the book falling on the floor.

At three in the morning, he heard a ringing. At first he thought it was the alarm clock, and rolled over to switch if off. But the ringing continued, and he finally realised it was the telephone.

Still half asleep, Jim picked it up and answered it. The call was from a doctor at the hospital.

"I'm sorry, Mr Robinson," the doctor said. "But I've some bad news for you. Your wife is dead."

Chapter 18

DEVASTATED with grief, Jim talked to the hospital staff, demanding to know what had happened. When he had left Anne the night before, she had been well and happy. How could she be dead in just a few short hours?

The doctors were sympathetic, but sorry. It was one of those one-in-a-million happenings, something that even modern medical science couldn't predict. A blood clot had worked loose from the pelvic region, and gone straight to the lungs. A nurse coming in with the baby to feed, had made the grim discovery.

Jim asked to see his wife, and was taken into the room where only a short time ago there had been joy and laughter. He sat down in the chair where Julie had nursed Lucy in her arms. The bassinet was no longer there, removed to the nursery.

Anne was lying with her eyes closed, almost

as though she were asleep. The room had been darkened, and the medical chart taken from the foot of her bed. As Jim looked down at her, Anne's face looked relaxed and peaceful, all the lines and tension gone from it. She looked like a teenager again.

Jim took one of Anne's hands in his. It felt cold . . . his first instinct was to put it against his cheek to warm it, but then he realised it was useless. As he sat there, silent, he saw she was wearing the gold cross and chain he'd given her for her birthday.

A sister came in and asked if he'd like anything — a cup of tea, some brandy? Jim shook his head.

The sister said it was terrible, all the hospital staff were upset about it. It had been the first death of a mother they'd ever had. And Mrs Robinson had been such a lovely lady.

Jim hardly heard what she was saying. The sister said he could visit his baby daughter any time he wanted, and quietly went out.

Baby daughter? In his grief, Jim had forgotten about Lucy. Now he almost resented her. If she hadn't been born, Anne would still be living.

Almost at once, he put the thought out of his mind. He couldn't take out his pain and anger on a small scrap of humanity, only a few days old. He'd been robbed of a wife — she was robbed of a mother she'd hardly had time to know.

Suddenly Jim broke down, sobbing uncontrollably.

"Oh, Anne," he wept. "Why did you have to leave me?"

*　　　*　　　*

There was a quiet family funeral, and Anne was buried in the local cemetery. The flowers on her coffin were white roses.

The hospital returned all Anne's personal possessions, including the gold chain and cross. Jim locked it away in a box, together with Anne's engagement ring and a few small pieces of jewellery. She was buried wearing the plain gold wedding ring Jim had given her thirteen years ago.

Lucy went from the hospital to a nursing home, until Jim could pick up the pieces of his life and decide what to do. Helen stayed on, looking after the other three children.

She never told Jim about David's new marriage proposal, nor the art scholarship to Paris. Right now, there were more important things to think about. And she delayed ringing David.

The day after the funeral, as Helen and Jim

sat in the living room quietly reading through letters and condolence cards from friends, Jim came to a decision.

He had four young motherless children dependent on him. They would need all the care and time he could give them. And there was still that mortgage on the house hanging over him.

"I'm pulling out from the business," he told Helen, as she sat darning socks. "Ross will have to find another partner."

"As soon as I can organise my affairs, I'm going back to my old job."

Chapter 19

JIM was normally a steady, easy going man of strong character who could cope with most things in life. But after Anne died, he fell into a deep depression.

He shut himself away in his bedroom, only coming out for meals. He was kind and loving with the children, but avoided all mention of their mother. It was left to Helen to explain it to them, and ease them through the pain of Anne's death.

Strangely, the children coped with it much better than their father. They cried, of course, especially Julie. But once they accepted it, they picked up the threads of their old lives . . . going to school, playing with friends, outings with the Ramsay boys.

Max and Maria were very supportive, and came over every day. But even with Max, Jim couldn't relax and unwind. There were no more beers shared together when Max came home from work. No more goodnatured banter. It was almost as if Jim had cut himself off from the world, and was unable to face the future.

Helen knew a certain amount of grief was healthy. It had taken her a long time to get over Bill's death. But she began to worry as the days went by and Jim showed no signs of returning to normal life.

In their room, Jim left all of Anne's things untouched. Her clothes hung in the wardrobe, her makeup and perfumes were still on the dressing table. The blue dress which Helen had given Anne for her birthday lay in its cardboard box, surrounded by tissue paper. There was even a half-completed shopping list, made up the day she was rushed to hospital. Once, when Helen started to tidy up some things, Jim had become very angry and stopped her. From then on, she left the room as it was.

But she didn't like going into it. It had the feel of a shrine, as if Jim felt by leaving all of Anne's things untouched he could still keep a part of her alive.

Ross Warner had rung a few times, but Jim had asked Helen to say he wasn't available. His explanation was that he couldn't cope right now with talking business.

Ross was very sympathetic and understanding. He told Helen there was no hurry, Jim could take his time. But in the next breath he added there were a few projects he'd like to discuss with him. Helen had the feeling that Ross was missing Jim's expertise, and anxious to get him back into working harness. She wondered what his reaction would be when he found out Jim planned to leave the business.

The crisis came to a head when Helen gave Jim the painting of Anne in the garden. Jim looked at it, and broke down again.

"What am I going to do, Helen?" he sobbed.

As she put her arms around him and tried to comfort him, Helen knew very clearly what she had to do herself. And she did it quickly.

She rang Lawrence Manning and told him she couldn't take up the scholarship. He was regretful, but understood her reasons. Unfortunately, he said, under the terms of the scholarship it couldn't be deferred. It would go to the next person on the list.

Then she tore up the telephone number David had given her.

That night, after the children had gone to bed, Helen got tough with Jim. She told him he must stop living in the past, and start thinking about the future. There were four children who needed him — now, more than ever before. They had already lost their mother. By shutting himself away, and not coming to terms with

Anne's death, Jim was robbing them of a father as well.

Helen told Jim she was prepared to give up her flat and move permanently into the Robinson house to help with the children and new baby. She would stay for as long as they needed her.

But there was one condition to her staying. When Anne had been alive, they had often talked about Jim's new business venture. Helen knew how excited Anne was about it, her pride that Jim would finally be his own boss. She was prepared to make sacrifices to help him . . the last thing she could have wanted was for Jim to give up.

"Stick with it, for Anne's sake," Helen pleaded. "It's what she would have wanted. Give it a chance to make it work."

Jim finally agreed, and Helen put her affairs in order. She sold most of her furniture, keeping just a few personal things. Then she packed her easel and paintings, and took one last look around the flat that had been her home since Bill died.

So many memories . . .

The day Anne and Jim had helped her move in. The weekends and school holidays, when the children came to stay with 'Gran'. The curtains she'd made herself. The wall she'd papered, the Chinese rug she had picked up at an auction.

And the first time David Barrington had come for coffee.

The memory of David was still very painful. Helen was surprised how much it hurt. This was the day he was flying to Canada. She looked at her watch — in less than an hour, his plane would be overhead.

She thought for one wild moment of having him paged at the airport, just so she could hear his voice again and say goodbye. Then her commonsense took over.

If they were never to see each other again, it should be a clean break. No second thoughts, no regrets.

Outside the building a taxi horn sounded. Helen picked up her suitcase, and without a backward glance walked out the door and into her new life.

A Selected List of Fiction Available from Mandarin Books

While every effort is made to keep prices low, it is sometimes necessary to increase prices at short notice. Mandarin Paperbacks reserves the right to show new retail prices on covers which may differ from those previously advertised in the text or elsewhere.

The prices shown below were correct at the time of going to press.

☐	7493 0003 5	**Mirage**	James Follett	£3.99
☐	7493 0005 1	**China Saga**	C. Y. Lee	£3.50
☐	7493 0009 4	**Larksghyll**	Constance Heaven	£2.99
☐	7493 0012 4	**The Falcon of Siam**	Axel Aylwen	£3.99
☐	7493 0018 3	**Daughter of the Swan**	Joan Juliet Buck	£3.50
☐	7493 0020 5	**Pratt of the Argus**	David Nobbs	£3.50
☐	7493 0025 6	**Here Today**	Zoë Fairbairns	£3.50

TV and Film Titles

☐	7493 0002 7	**The Bill III**	John Burke	£2.99
☐	7493 0055 8	**Neighbours I**	Marshall/Kolle	£2.99
☐	423 02020 X	**Bellman and True**	Desmond Lowden	£2.50
☐	416 13972 8	**Why the Whales Came**	Michael Morpurgo	£2.50
☐	7493 0017 5	**Adventures of Baron Munchausen**	McKeown/Gilliam	£2.99

All these books are available at your bookshop or newsagent, or can be ordered direct from the publisher. Just tick the titles you want and fill in the form below.

Mandarin Paperbacks, Cash Sales Department, PO Box 11, Falmouth, Cornwall TR10 9EN.

Please send cheque or postal order, no currency, for purchase price quoted and allow the following for postage and packing:

UK	55p for the first book, 22p for the second book and 14p for each additional book ordered to a maximum charge of £1.75.
BFPO and Eire	55p for the first book, 22p for the second book and 14p for each of the next seven books, thereafter 8p per book.
Overseas Customers	£1.00 for the first book plus 25p per copy for each additional book.

NAME (Block Letters) ....

ADDRESS ....

....